# Citadel Securities Duet

## Ash Henry

# If You're Mine

by Ash Henry

# CHAPTER ONE
## *Gideon*

"There's no one I trust more than you, Blake. I need your help."

Trust the senator to get right to the point. I step into the small office and close the door, shutting out the clink of glasses and loud conversations of the Double Tap bar. My business partner, Derek, is sitting behind the desk with his boots kicked up and his tattooed fingers laced behind his neck.

Two years ago, we were in the same combat unit and discharged out together. Within a month, we'd relocated to New Orleans and started Citadel Securities. We now own the building, Double Tap, and Arcane Brew, the coffee shop next door.

Derek's eyebrows raise, silently asking why I'm using his office for a call instead of going to the Citadel office on the floor above.

I would have, but the phone rang right after I came downstairs to check inventory on some gear and the hair on the back of my neck stood up. I didn't recognize the number, but I knew I needed to take the call.

"How can I help you, Senator?" *And how the fuck did you get my personal cell number?*

The older man gusts out a heavy sigh and I hear what sounds like a chair creaking, as if he sat heavily in it. "There's an important vote on the hill two days from now. It's supposed to be top secret, but clearly word has gotten out."

"In my experience, the best way to let everyone know what's going on is to label something top secret." Especially where the government is concerned. Damn bunch of chatty hens.

The senator chokes out a strangled laugh. "You're probably right."

I've only met the man once. Six years ago in Afghanistan when we rescued him and a few of his aids from insurgents. They'd taken Mayfield and the others hostage for four hours before my team infiltrated and freed them.

"I pride myself on voting by my principles, Blake, which often makes me unpopular on either side of the aisle. The pressure on this vote is tremendous. All I can say is that it involves spending for national defense. Party lines are split, which leaves me and another senator as swing votes." The phone rustles, and when he speaks again, he sounds tired. "Someone got wind of the vote. This afternoon, I received what I'm told is a very credible threat. If I don't publicly admit that I'm voting against the bill, they will kidnap my daughter. The FBI has a few leads on who could be behind the threats, but can't narrow it down in time."

"Damn."

"I know you're no longer in the service, but I also know what you did for me and my aids that day. I just learned that you are in New Orleans, which is a godsend. Amber's in college there. I need you to pick her up and protect her before..." He clears his throat and when he speaks again, his voice is strained. "Before something happens to her."

"So you don't intend to make a statement?" I need to be clear of his intentions.

"I won't surrender to terrorists. But I can't risk my daughter's safety. Please, Gideon. She's my only child."

"I'll take care of it personally. No one will get near her." I'm already running through a list of preparations and alternative plans. "Where can I find her?"

The relief in his voice is palpable. "Her last class ends at five p.m. She usually goes home to study after that. I'll text you the details and tell her you're coming. Keep me in the loop."

"The fewer who know, the better, sir. Trust me. If you get any updates from the kidnappers, call. My man, Derek, will get the information to me."

Derek glares at me.

I shrug. He's here and the others aren't. He gets the job of go-between.

He shakes his head and flips me off.

The silent communication buoys my mood. We went through hell and back during the years we served together in Delta Force. There are few men I trust more. Despite his denial, I can count on him.

The senator sputters in anger. "Amber is my only child. I need to know she's safe."

I pinch the bridge of my nose and reach for patience. Can't blame a man for being afraid for his daughter. "I'll keep her safe. Notify my office once the vote is complete and I'll bring her home." That seems to mollify the man, and we finalize the last few details.

"Senator?" Derek asks after I've disconnected the call.

"Remember Congressman Mayfield? We pulled him out of Afghanistan when his goodwill tour, or whatever the fuck it was, went sideways?"

He snorts and reaches for a cup of coffee I hadn't noticed on the desk. Double Tap's office has just enough room for the desk, filing cabinet, and a couple of chairs. The French doors leading out to our private courtyard are its best feature.

"I remember." Derek sips his coffee. "They shouldn't have been there."

There's no arguing about that. "It's Senator Mayfield now. Someone's putting pressure on him to vote against some top-secret security bill. They've threatened his family."

A muscle in Derek's jaw twitches, and he runs a hand through his auburn hair.

The look on his face reflects the fury in my gut. We both know how this could end. We've seen it far too often, both in the service and as civilians once we started Citadel. I have to get to the senator's daughter in time. If the kidnappers grab Amber first, she's as good as dead.

Derek turns his troubled gaze on the courtyard. "They'll never stop, will they?"

"No. That's why we do what we do." My phone trills with an incoming text. I open the screen, expecting more information from Mayfield about his daughter and her habits. Instead, I spot the name of an old friend from high school who now works with my sister. I almost ignore it, but Trish never contacts me. It's odd enough to make me check the message.

*Trish: Gideon, I gotta talk to you about Harmony right away. Call me.*

Dammit, I don't have time for this. I type out a quick reply, certain this can wait. I love my sister, but Harmony has a knack for seeing the world as one big, beautiful place and worrying the shit out of everyone who knows it's not.

Trish's reply is instant.

I dial her number.

An hour later, my truck is packed and ready, yet I'm stuck here, waiting for my buddy Caleb. I check my watch for the fifth time in ten minutes and try to calm my racing heart.

I hate this. My sister is in trouble and I can't do a goddamn thing about it because I just committed to the senator that I would personally guard his daughter. I could send someone else to protect Amber, but if anything went wrong, and he was forced into a vote he clearly doesn't want to make, the lives of tens of thousands could be affected.

There's no good decision here. I grip the back of my neck. My only option is to send Caleb to help Harmony. We grew up together in a tiny mountain town in Montana. He spent more time at our house than his. If I can't be there for Harmony, Caleb's the next best thing. I have to believe that sending him will be enough to protect her. Anything else is unacceptable.

# Chapter Two

## *Amber*

*There's a security agent coming to protect you. Do everything he tells you.*

*Amber?*

*Call me when you get these.*

I'm crossing the quad on the way to the parking lot after my last class, trying not to sweat too much from the sticky summer heat when I check the texts that came in over the last hour. Growing up in Texas, you'd think I'd be used to humid summers, but I swear they're worse in the Mississippi Delta. It's like its own ecosystem of muggy, buggy, and sweaty. The texts from my dad stops me cold. One second I'm too warm and the next, I feel like an iceberg just lodged in my chest.

I'm twenty-two and this is my last year of college. I shouldn't be shackled by my parents anymore. Not like this.

My phone dings with another text while I'm still reeling from the first. I want to shove the phone in my backpack and pretend I never heard it, but I can't. I already saw the first message and he'll see that it's been read.

I wait until I'm at my car before reading the second text.

*His name is Gideon Blake.*

Why can't they see that I'm an adult now? I wonder if my mother is somehow behind this. She's usually the one that hires the bodyguards and private detectives. My roommates tease me about never dating, but who wants to kiss a boy if a photographer could pop out of the bushes at any moment to report back to your parents? It's insane. Part of me wonders if *they're* insane. I get that my father is a U.S. Senator, but it's not like I'm the president's daughter and need Secret Service to go to the bathroom with me.

I type out and delete several replies.

Another message comes through before I can settle on one to send. It's a picture of a guy in his thirties, maybe, wearing a charcoal gray suit. His hair is dark brown and his face is rugged. Stern. Definitely not bad looking. I guess if I have to have a security guard, one who looks like him would make it worth it.

*Do exactly as he says, Pumpkin.*

I groan as I realize that there's no getting through to my dad. He rarely texts me. To send me this many in one day means he's super focused on something and whatever it is involves me. My finals are starting, so I'm just going to be home studying anyway. The guy is going to be bored out of his mind. I hope he likes to watch a lot of TV.

*Okay, I will. But why?* I text back.

A minute passes while I'm waiting for my dad to reply.

Two... Three.

I can't do this. Shoving the phone in my pocket, I slide into the car and drive the few blocks back to my apartment.

None of my roommates' vehicles are there, which means I can study in peace. They're nice, but sometimes being around them makes me feel... not exactly left out. Just... different. Their lives are a rotation of who's dating who, what party is next, and who borrowed their mini-dress. That's not me.

My parents never allowed me to date, and our security system ensured I could never sneak out. I couldn't even spend the night with friends for a typical teen sleepover unless they came to my house. I've never even kissed a guy.

Since I was seven, they've dictated every part of my life. Who my friends are, monitoring my time online, not even any extracurricular activities at school. I thought attending college in a different state would have changed things, but it's not enough. The only way I'll escape is to graduate and support myself with a job they approve of. Anything less and they'll find a way to drag me back to Texas.

God, I need to be free of them for good. They mean well, but I can't live that sheltered life anymore. I'm so close. Just three more finals and I'll have my business degree.

Right as I reach for my backpack, my phone buzzes in my pocket. It's probably my father brushing off my question. I pull the phone out and check the screen, stomach sinking when I see my mother's picture.

*Don't question your father. Just do as he says or I will have that bodyguard bring you straight here. I told your father we should do that anyway, but he's refusing. Give the man any trouble and I will come get you myself. We should never have let you go to that school.*

I see the three dots indicating that she's writing more and type out a quick reply to head off the rant she's starting.

*Okay, mom. He can be my shadow everywhere I go. I won't let him out of my sight.*

That should be easy enough, since I'm not planning to go anywhere. Grabbing my backpack, I lock the car and head toward my apartment, dreading my mother's response. Maybe I'll order a pity pizza and ice cream. Nothing like comfort food after dealing with my parents.

Those three dots on her text are taunting me. What else can—something slams into my back hard enough to knock the phone from my hand. It bounces off the sidewalk and the screen shatters.

"Don't scream," a nasally male voice says in my ear as hard arms band about my chest. My backpack is ripped off me and I hear it hit the ground.

Oh god. My body freezes up and my heart races.

A second man with swarthy skin steps in front of me. He grips my hair in his fist and yanks my head back, then holds up a phone. "That's her."

*Oh god, oh god, oh god.* I didn't get my stern bodyguard yet. When was he supposed to meet me? My dad never said. Who are these men?

"Let's move." He releases me and turns away, apparently expecting my captor to follow.

My brain finally connects with my body and I struggle against the man holding me. "HEL—"

A rough hand slaps over my mouth, cutting off my cry. "Shut up, bitch. Come quietly and we won't hurt you."

Do they really think that will work? Like I'm going to believe them and go meekly? I stomp down on the man's foot as hard as I can and throw my weight forward, trying to break his grip.

He snarls and lifts me off my feet, calling out something in Spanish.

The second man swings around and grabs my ankles.

I kick and thrash and bite at the hand covering my mouth. Is the entire apartment complex empty? Where is everyone? A tear slips from my eye when one arm tightens around me and the hand from my mouth drops to my throat and squeezes.

I claw at his hand, but his grip is like iron. "Why?" I gasp.

He ignores me and starts for a black panel van.

A hysterical laugh escapes when I see it. Of course it's a van. Kidnappers don't drive anything else, do they? It's standard equipment. Like duct tape and rope and, oh my god, I don't want to die. I'm so close to graduating.

I kick at the man still holding my feet and manage to get one leg free.

There's a hard jolt at my back, and the kidnapper behind me grunts in my ear. Suddenly, he lets go. I land on my ass on the sidewalk. Ouch.

The other releases my ankle and pulls a gun from his waistband.

No!

There's a blur from behind me, then someone large is there. The thud of flesh hitting flesh makes me flinch. It's over almost as soon as it starts. Two punches, a knee, and a kick, and my kidnappers lie unmoving on the ground.

What just happened?

A tanned hand appears in my line of vision, offering me help up. I follow the hand up a muscled arm to a rugged face with a firm jaw covered by a dark five o'clock shadow, and stern forest green eyes that look as if they've seen a thousand battles. A black shirt molds to his chest and black cargo pants hang low on his trim hips. Strength and power radiate from him like a physical presence I feel to my core.

I squeeze my thighs together at the tingle going through my lady parts. My heart skips a beat and I can hardly breathe.

My babysitter, Gideon Blake, has arrived.

# Chapter Three
## *Gideon*

She's in shock.

Amber stares at me with wide eyes, her chest heaving, and covers her mouth with her palm.

I've got to get her out of here, but she has to understand that I'm here to help her, and right now, I'm not sure where she's at. Tucking the gun I just took off the kidnapper in the waistband of my cargo pants, I squat down to eye-level with her.

"Amber, my name is Gid—"

Tires squeal and the van I clocked idling nearby roars up and slams to a halt. Three men jump out and run toward us.

Shit. There's no time to hide her.

Two head for me, while the third angles around a car, probably hoping to grab her while I'm distracted. Not happening.

I pull Amber to her feet and tuck her behind me. With a hand on her hip, I back us up a few steps until the wall of the apartment complex is behind us. It forces the three men to go through me if they want her. My kind of odds.

My blood is already pumping from the first fight and I can't keep the smile from my face as my opponents near. The Senator's daughter brushes her fingers against my lower back, telling me without words that she's with me.

The fight is fast and intense. Two of the men have combat training, probably ex-military. Unfortunately for them, Delta teams learn fighting tactics on a whole different level than regular service members.

Less than two minutes of fun and all three are incapacitated.

When I turn back to Amber, she's pale and shaky. From the information Senator Mayfield sent, I know she's twenty-two and finishing college. The picture he sent didn't do her justice. Even scared out of her mind, the woman's gorgeous. Long strands of auburn hair have fallen out of a messy bun to frame her oval face and wide, honey brown eyes. She's on the thin side with curvy hips, just begging for my hands. The floral halter top she's wearing emphasizes her perfect breasts and all that pretty skin. She looks soft, and far too tempting for a man who is just supposed to protect her. Shit.

I clear my throat. "I'm Gideon Blake. Your father sent me."

She gives a jerky nod. "Wh-who are they?"

"Bad people who are looking for leverage." That's as sugar-coated as I can make it. No need to scare her further.

"Kidnappers," she whispers.

I cup her shoulder in one hand, feeling satiny skin beneath my fingertips, and lean down a few inches to meet her eyes, needing her to understand. "I'm not going to let anyone hurt you, Amber. You're safe with me."

She glances at the slumped bodies of the five men around us. When she looks back at me, the tension flows out of her body. Then she steps forward, wraps her arms around me, and buries her head against my neck.

Warmth fills my chest. Tentatively, I wrap my arms around her. I shouldn't be hugging a client. It breaks all sorts of rules. Right now, all I can feel is an overwhelming protectiveness for this woman and an alarming sense that she belongs right here, by my heart.

We don't have time for this. More men could show up any minute when these guys don't check in, and yet, I can't let her go. The way she fits against me... Her soft curves press against my body in all the right places, and she's just tall enough to brush her lips over my neck. She tucks into my body just right.

Her breath sighs out against my skin and my cock hardens almost painfully. The feeling is so intense, it pushes through the haze of whatever this instinct is. My focus must be on protecting her, not bedding her.

*Get it together, Blake.*

I unwind her arms from around me and take a step back. "We have to go, honey." The endearment slips out unbidden, inspired by those honey-colored eyes. *Goddammit, Blake. Get. It. Together.* "There may be more nearby. I'll take you to a safe house until this vote with your father is over."

She stiffens. "A vote. I should have known it was political." Then her forehead furrows. "I can't leave. I have finals. These are my last classes. If I miss them, I won't graduate."

"Sorry, Miss Mayfield." The distance created by the propriety of using her last name is needed, but saying it feels wrong. "Someone sent five men to take you hostage. Anyone with that kind of manpower usually has no problem finding more."

She growls. "I hate politics. Fine. Let me grab some clothes and we can go to your safe house."

I'm already shaking my head. "No time. We need to leave now. We'll stop on the way and buy whatever you need."

"That makes no sense. We're right here." She waves at the apartment window one floor up.

"Listen to me. I don't know who's after you, but I do know that they won't stop until they can use you against your father. I don't want to have to fight our way out of a second-story apartment with only one exit if they show up before we can leave." I take her by the shoulders and steer her toward where I'm parked. "So get in my truck and we'll pick up what you need on the way."

She huffs out an aggravated sigh and stomps toward my vehicle, leaning down to swipe up her backpack and phone.

"Leave the phone."

"But—"

I gently take it from her hand, then toss it at the nearest patch of grass. "They can track you through it."

Amber frowns at it, and finally nods.

She's not happy, that much is clear. But she's safe for now, and that's what matters.

Soon, we're driving through the crowded streets of New Orleans, taking a circuitous route to make sure we aren't tailed. I don't breathe easy until we're on the highway, heading north into Mississippi.

"Why is this happening?" she asks.

"Your father didn't tell you?"

"I asked, but he didn't reply. Just my mother, threatening to have you take me back to Texas if I didn't do everything you instructed."

Hearing that her mother is overprotective in this situation isn't a surprise. I'd be concerned if she *wasn't*. "Is that where you're from?"

Amber nods, then turns to face me. "You work for my father. Do you do everything he tells you to do?"

I steal a glance at her. "That's not how this works."

"Then how does it work? I... I can't go back to Texas." Her hands clench into fists in her lap.

The raspy strain to her voice sends an arrow straight through the armor I just erected to keep her at bay. The need to protect her, to comfort her, is overwhelming. The control over my emotions that I spent years honing disappeared the second I saw her. I reach over and cover her hands. "He hired me to make sure those men didn't grab you, and to keep you safe until after the Senate vote. How I do so is my decision. My clients don't dictate the security parameters."

She unclenches a fist, and my hand slips into hers. It feels natural. Way too good, and I know that I've already crossed a line. The trouble is, I'm not certain I can restrain myself. When I think I have my emotions under control, one little frown from her is all it takes to blast through those barriers. It's like something inside recognizes her as the missing part of me. If I believed in soul mates, or love at first sight, maybe it would make sense.

I don't and it doesn't. Not sure where that leaves me except straight up fucked. This woman is far too young for me, her father is my client, and getting close to her breaks every rule I personally created for operatives at Citadel.

"Why don't you want to go back to Texas?" I have to get my mind off this shit or I might do something I'll regret. Like pull over right here and kiss the hell out of her.

"Because my mother will never let me leave again. Not after this."

I slide another glance at her. She's looking out the window. Her skin is too pale. "Why wouldn't she let you leave?"

She finally turns to me and the bleakness in her expression slays me. "Because when I was seven, my best friend was kidnapped and never came home."

Pieces click into place. Her mother's overprotectiveness and her father's desperation to know where his daughter is make a lot more sense. "This must be her worst nightmare. But once she sees that you're safe—"

Amber shakes her head. "As a teen, I was never allowed to go out with friends or date. I thought things would be better when I left for college. I thought I'd finally be free to do what I wanted. I quickly realized that I couldn't risk even trying to date because my mom kept hiring investigators and bodyguards to keep an eye on me. They reported back to her about everything. When she heard about a frat party my roommates dragged me to, she hired movers to come pack my stuff. Thankfully, I convinced my dad that I hadn't wanted to go to the party and he got her to cancel the move." She swipes at her damp cheeks. "God, I was so close to graduating."

My chest feels tight at the hollow sound of her voice. I can't imagine being raised under a microscope like that. I've seen a full range of reactions from the parents of kidnapped kids. I understand the fear that can take hold after they get their child back. But the kidnapped child wasn't Amber. Her mother's actions seem extreme. Now that there's been an attempt to take Amber, I wonder how much worse her mother's reaction will be.

"Maybe you should just take me back to Texas."

"No. We keep going as planned. Once this is over, I'll take you back to school." Maybe I can pull a few strings to arrange make up exams for her. For now, I need to find a place to stop for supplies before we head to the cabin. A few days in front of a cozy fire, surrounded by nature, might bring that smile back. I hope so.

Goddamn, I'm screwed.

# CHAPTER FOUR
## *Amber*

What does one wear when hiding from kidnappers? Jeans? Sweats? I swallow, my throat aching from the bruises left by one of them, and flip through the rack of pants in front of me. We drove for over three hours after crossing into Mississippi and eventually stopped at this superstore to buy clothes and food.

All I remember from the drive was a blur of green scenery until the sun sank behind the hills in a beautiful display of pinks and purples. It took me an hour to stop shaking.

Kidnapping. I just can't... What if Gideon had been five minutes later? What if they find us but they bring more men? Or what if they force my dad to do what they want? Who will be hurt because of me?

A warm hand settles against my lower back and the smell of cedar surrounds me. Gideon. That simple touch settles the rioting fear that keeps creeping in, flooding my mind with 'what ifs'.

"The store is closing in a few minutes, honey. We need to go."

I haven't picked anything to wear and I know we've been here for half an hour. "Um..."

"What size?"

I tell him, and he selects a couple pairs of jeans and puts them in the cart, then guides me over toward the women's shirts. With his help, I find a few that will work. It's harder to buy bras and underwear in front of him. My cheeks flame the entire time. No one has even seen me in just my underwear, and yet it feels so much more intimate to tell Gideon my bra size.

When I opt for the simple cotton I normally choose. He adds a beautiful black lace set to the cart.

"Gideon. I'm buying clothes to go into hiding, not model lingerie."

He grunts, and it sounds pained. "No reason why you can't wear something pretty."

The lace is silky to the touch. "I've never owned anything sexy. I've wanted to, but the little money I have goes to food. It seems too extravagant."

His fingers brush over my lips to silence the objection. His voice is a low purr when he says, "You're allowed to feel beautiful no matter the circumstances, honey."

My belly swoops at his seductive whisper. The thought of wearing them makes me smile and I wonder, would he ever want to see me in them?

By the time the announcement comes over the speakers that the store is closing, I've managed to add toiletries and a carry bag that will hold everything. We hurry through the grocery section, only getting enough food to last us a day or two. Gideon said it might draw someone's attention to get more. We can explain my clothes as lost luggage from the airlines.

He hasn't left my side for even a minute. When my dad first texted, I remember thinking that I didn't need a babysitter. I expected a big, bossy man in a suit who wore dark glasses, hovered over my shoulder, and frowned a lot. The same type of guardian my parents usually hired. Gideon charged in like a superhero, and I can't help but feel like I won the bodyguard lottery. I probably shouldn't have thrown myself into his arms after he beat up my attackers. I half expected him to push me away. Instead, he wrapped me in those strong arms and made my world right again.

The stern man I saw in that text photo is nothing like the one that held me. He fought brutally and I couldn't take my eyes off the raw power in his movements as he punched, kicked, and flipped my kidnappers, leaving them in a broken heap. Then he held my hand, and I saw a tender side that I never expected. I've never met anyone like him, and I know that I've only scratched the surface of Gideon Blake. I have so many questions about him, and yet I can barely make a decision on what kind of pants to buy.

"I swear I'm not normally such a mess." We're at the checkout counter. A tired woman in her fifties with purple extensions is ringing up our purchases. Her purple eyebrows creep up when she looks at me.

Gideon takes cash from his wallet and pays her. "I don't think you're a mess."

What does he think of me? The man has the poker face of a pro. The best face period. The dark scruff of hair on his jaw highlights his cheeks and firm lips. His eyes are the deepest green I've ever seen and I want to run my hands through his hair to see if it's as thick as it looks.

He loads the bags into the cart and reaches for my hand, lacing our fingers together. I know he does it so that we'll look like a normal couple to any observers. It doesn't stop the explosion of butterflies in my tummy or the way my heart foolishly flips.

Bright lights shine down on the nearly empty parking lot when we exit the store. Gideon parked the truck right under the closest one, giving us a clear view around the vehicle.

"The cabin's not far," he says after he's loaded the bags into the back seat of the truck. He opens my door. "You hungry?"

"Not yet."

"You will be." He scans the parking lot and then steps closer to me. His hand comes up as if to cup my cheek, but he hesitates.

I need that touch. I need him.

Before he can change his mind, I take his hand and guide it to my cheek, pressing my palm over his. I don't know if it's just that he rescued me or if it's something more, but every time he touches me, it feels right. Like his skin on mine is the only thing that makes sense in this crazy world. When he touches me, I don't care that he's older or that he's guarding me, or that I don't really even know him. All I know is that he's what I need.

Our eyes meet. He brings his other hand up to hold my face and draws me closer. "So soft," he murmurs as his thumb strokes my skin.

The connection between us is so strong that it's hard to breathe. I've never been kissed before and I want him to be my first. His chest is hard beneath my hands and I can feel every muscle under his thin T-shirt. Our lips are a breath apart.

I push to my toes to close the distance. The feather-light brush of my lips against his, breathing in his scent, and hearing the deep rumble of his moan floods my body with desire. He slants his mouth over mine and deepens the kiss.

The tender way he holds my face is at odds with the hungry melding of our mouths. He strokes his tongue with mine, pressing me back against the side of the truck. I'm lost in the feelings swimming through me. I never knew kissing could be like this. Every place he touches feels as if it's on fire, burning me from the inside out.

Gideon grips my ass in his big hands and grinds his lower body against my hips. The hard length of him rubs just the right place between my thighs. I can't help the moan that slips out. More. I need more.

He freezes, lips hovering over mine.

I chase his mouth and kiss him again, but he doesn't kiss me back. His eyes are squeezed closed as if he's in pain.

"Gideon?"

When his eyes snap open, his face smooths out, and I'm staring at a stranger.

He drags in a deep breath, then steps back. "I can't."

The sudden change feels like a slap in the face. My stomach bottoms out and ice slides through my veins. Did I read him wrong? Did I make myself believe he wants what I want so I wouldn't have to think about kidnappers and losing my freedom? God, I'm such an idiot. Of course he doesn't really want to kiss me. I'm at least ten years younger than him, still in college, and can't even pretend that I have my life together.

A shard of pain stabs my heart. I climb into the truck, crossing my arms over my stomach as if I can hold in the hurt. And that's dumb too. I shouldn't feel wrecked by his rejection.

Gideon takes my seatbelt and snaps it around me, then gently moves my hands out from under it. He's silent as he closes my door, then climbs in behind the wheel.

His face is void of emotion and I don't want to see it. All I want now is to be alone. To curl up in bed and forget this day ever happened.

"You're vulnerable, honey. I won't take advantage of that," he says into the darkness of the cab several minutes later. We're on a one lane road winding through a forest, the night pitch black around us.

I won't cry. My nails bite into my palms, the sharp sting grounding me. Apparently, I lied in the store. I *am* this much of a mess. "Thanks."

"Don't thank me. Not when I hurt you in the process."

I want to deny that he did, but I can't. Uncomfortable silence falls between us.

There's a break in the tree line ahead. We turn onto a dirt path that ends in a small clearing. The cabin looks homey, with flower boxes in the window full of sunny yellow flowers, lace curtains, and a lamp burning in the window.

Gideon parks and we gather our bags. The inside of the cabin is clean and bright, with that farmhouse style so popular right now and wide, wood plank floors. There's a simple kitchen with a table, a squashy looking couch in front of the fireplace, and a staircase that most likely leads to the bedrooms.

Everything a person could need to hide from kidnappers.

# Chapter Five
## Gideon

I did the right thing and I still feel like I fucked up. I stuff a few more pieces of old newspaper under the logs in the fireplace and adjust them with the poker, trying to get the fire to light. The cabin is warm enough now that we don't need it, but I need something productive to do to keep from pulling Amber back into my arms. I toss the poker aside when the fire catches and run a hand down my face.

Jesus, the way Amber shut down after that kiss is gutting me. She has no idea how close I came to throwing my honor out the window for a full taste of her. That feathery brush of mouths sent a rush of fire through me that made it hard to breathe. Her sexy body fit perfect against me, where her hips nestled with mine, and the need to get my hands on her skin, to cup her breasts and feel the slickness of her pussy nearly put me over the edge. I was half a heartbeat from lifting her into the truck and stripping her, when her eager little moan finally penetrated the haze of lust.

I'm supposed to be fucking protecting this girl and instead, I'm making out with her in an empty parking lot where anyone could come upon us. My actions shamed me. Taking advantage of a vulnerable woman under my care? That's not who I thought I was.

I've spent the better part of my life protecting others. Getting involved with a client compromises my ability to do my job. I know that. And yet the intense protectiveness I feel toward her is overwhelming. I can still feel that damn kiss. The moment I held her in my arms, there was only one thought in my head: *Mine.*

A creak on the stairs draws me out of my spinning thoughts. I stand and turn to find Amber coming down the stairs with a towel and a new flannel shirt in her hands. I frown.

"The fire should keep the cabin from getting cold tonight. I don't think you'll need anything that heavy to sleep in."

She bites her bottom lip, leaving it red and plump. My cock throbs at the sight.

"I forgot to get pajamas. This is the only thing I had. It'll be okay. I won't take a hot shower."

Fuck that. She needs to relax and the hot shower will do her good. I haven't been up to the bedrooms for anything more than a cursory check to make sure the cabin was safe and all the windows were locked, so my duffel is sitting on the floor by the sofa. I dig through it and pull out one of my T-shirts. "Here. You can wear one of mine. I have extra."

Amber takes the soft green shirt from me. "Are you sure?"

"I told you I'd take care of you. That includes pajama service."

A tiny smile tugs at one corner of her mouth and I feel like a goddamn hero.

"Go warm up, honey. I'll make sure things are secure."

Amber nods and slips into the bathroom.

It's well after midnight by the time I get my own shower in. I made myself a sandwich and tried to feed Amber but she just wanted to sleep. I check in with Derek and learn that the attempted kidnapping made the news. Someone's doorbell camera recorded the fight and got a perfect shot of Amber's terrified face. Derek had to field calls from both of her parents and chews me out for not checking in sooner.

Grumpy bastard. He'll calm them down though. He always does.

Tossing the phone aside, I settle on the couch. There's a second bedroom upstairs, but one look at that comfortable bed earlier and I knew I couldn't risk lying down. I'm tired, but I need to remain alert. Here, I can slip into a light doze but still be aware of noises that seem out of place.

My thoughts turn to the beautiful woman upstairs. She did well today. She never fell apart, even though she shed a few tears. I admire that strength. It's what draws me to her, not just her looks. Yes, she's gorgeous with all that thick auburn hair in a messy bun that begs me to pull it free and run my fingers through it. Her curves are perfect. Plump breasts, small waist, and rounded hips. There's also an innocence to her that appeals to me.

From what she told me about her up-bringing, I had the sense that she was inexperienced. But then she kissed me, and that tentative brush of her mouth, the knowledge that I might be the first one to taste her lips, hit me on a level that's almost caveman. I want to be her first in *everything*. The thought of those men getting their hands on her makes me want to throw her over my shoulder and declare to the world that she's mine.

I'm losing my fucking mind.

"Gideon?"

Amber's soft voice floats down to me from the top of the stairs. I can still hear the slight rasp from where that asshole choked her and it makes me want to rip his throat out. Jesus.

"What is it, honey?" The endearment slips out easier every time and I'm done fighting myself over it. Less than twelve hours with this woman and I've turned into a feral fucking caveman using sweet endearments. Thank god Derek and Caleb aren't here to witness this meltdown.

She comes downstairs and I realize that I gave her my green Army T-shirt that I've had since basic. The damn thing's been washed so many times that it's thin and almost threadbare, but I like it because it's soft. Draped over Amber's curves? I'm never getting rid of it. Holy shit. My cock hardens so fast it hurts.

"I can't sleep." She rubs her arms. "Every noise keeps jolting me awake."

"Want to come sit with me for a while? Maybe I can bore you with a story until you fall asleep."

Amber laughs and almost skips over to the couch. "I'd love to hear a story."

I scoot over to the end of the couch to give her room, but she sits down beside me, so close her shoulder brushes mine. I have to distract myself or I will pick up where we left off earlier. "What do you want to hear?"

"How did you start protecting people?"

"I joined the military when I was eighteen with my friend, Caleb. He needed out of our small town and I went with him. We spent almost fifteen years in the service. That's where I met your father."

"In Washington?"

"Afghanistan."

Amber turns to me, eyes wide. "He never told me what happened, but I overheard him tell my mom that he and his aids were rescued from terrorists by special forces. Was that you?"

I nod. One of her father's aids didn't make it. His murder is one of hundreds that are still with me. If we'd been half an hour earlier, could we have saved him?

She launches forward against my chest, winding her arms around my neck, and presses a kiss to my cheek. "Thank you. Thank you for saving him. I don't know what I would have done without him. He's the only one that... that stands between me and my mom."

I don't know what to say to that. I hold her to me and press a kiss to her temple. "My buddy, Derek and I, started Citadel Securities. It allows us to use our skills to help people."

"What happened to your friend, Caleb?"

"He works with us. He's protecting my sister right now." The glare he gave me when he realized that he'd have to return to White Falls nags at me. I hope he faces those demons while he's there.

Amber yawns and snuggles closer. "What's your sister like?"

It takes me a moment to respond. Having her in my lap is not doing anything to help my hard-on. I adjust her so it's not pressing into her hip. "You'd like

Harmony. She's bright and happy, and nothing like me."

She hums and shifts her hip back against my dick. Her breath fans my ear and she says, "But I like you, Gideon."

# Chapter Six

## Amber

His eyes search mine.

Does he see how much I still want him? I don't move, half afraid he'll reject me again.

"I like you too, honey," he whispers. Then his mouth covers mine.

The kiss is soft, exploratory. He takes his time, letting me adjust to the press of his lips. It's beautiful and amazing, and not enough.

My hands go into his hair and instinctively pull him closer. His kiss turns harder, hungry, making me gasp. Then he deepens the kiss. His tongue strokes against mine and I'm suddenly drowning in delicious sensation. I feel that stroke of his tongue everywhere. My nipples harden into points, every brush of his soft shirt against my skin sending pulses of pleasure to my core until I'm wet and needy.

He cups the back of my head, holding me in place, and plunders my mouth.

I can't sit still. My hips writhe against his hard bulge. I can't get enough of this feeling. This ache. I want to see him and touch him. Taste him. Take his hard cock in my body until there's nothing separating us. It's crazy and I'm here for it.

Gideon's large hand slides up my bare thigh and slips under the edge of his T-shirt. "I love seeing my clothes on you, honey. The only thing better would be seeing you out of them," he murmurs against my mouth. His hand slips between my thighs, pressing against my core. "Jesus, you're not wearing any panties."

I gasp when his fingers slide through my folds. No one's ever touched me this intimately. It's surprising and addicting. Hot and mind-blowing. I never knew a simple touch could stir all these feelings.

Gideon leans his forehead against mine and slowly pulls his hand away.

"Wait..." I grab his wrist. Why is he stopping?

"I shouldn't have touched you, Amber. My job is to protect you. Not make you orgasm on my hand or my tongue."

I clench my thighs against the erotic images he paints. Yes. I need that. "I want you to touch me." I try to pull his hand back to my pussy, but he resists.

"It wouldn't be right."

Nothing has ever felt so right. Doesn't he feel it too? Did he misinterpret my surprise, thinking I was scared or repulsed? "Gideon, please. I—"

One look at him and I know he's closed himself off once more. There's no emotion in his eyes. Like a wall slammed down behind them, letting nothing of what he's feeling show through. I really, really wish I could do that.

I try to slip off his lap, but he locks an arm around my waist.

"Just rest. I've got you. We'll talk about this tomorrow."

"No. I—"

He threads his fingers through my hair, gripping the strands to stop my struggle. "Amber, I'm not fucking you the first day I meet you. You deserve better than that. It's been a rough fucking day. *Please*, honey. Give us both a chance to process this."

Holding me like he is, I can't look away. So I get a front-row seat to the flashes of frustration and longing that slip past the wall he's erected.

It's enough. For now.

I settle against him, lay my head on his shoulder, and stare at the fire. Maybe Gideon's right. Maybe in the light of day, I'll realize that this was all just the fear spilling over and everything will look different...

It doesn't.

I wake up on the couch, alone and grumpy. Gideon is nowhere to be found. People still want to kidnap me, my parents want to lock me in a tower like Rapunzel, and I want a man who doesn't want me. Nothing's. Changed.

I use the bathroom and brush my teeth, then stomp into the kitchen and bang some pans around just to feel better while I make breakfast. The eggs and toast fill my grumbling tummy and take the edge off my anger. For once in my life, I want to truly have a decision in my future. I thought college would be that choice but it looks as if that's been taken from me too.

You know what? No. "That's it, Universe. No more letting other people interfere. Kidnappers, controlling parents, gorgeous and completely unavailable bodyguards who kiss like they want to devour me and still hold me at arm's length... I'm done letting them have their say. It's only me and what I want for my life."

The universe answers with a steady thwacking noise from outside.

It's kind of anti-climatic.

I follow the noise to the window. Gideon is in the yard, swinging an ax like a sexy woodsman. He's shirtless, and the defined ridges of muscle glisten with a sheen of sweat. It takes far too long to unstick my tongue from the roof of my mouth.

I'm not sure if the Universe is thumbing its nose at me or telling me to go for it. Since it's my life, I decide it's the latter, and rush upstairs to pull some jeans and shoes on. I grab a bottle of water, and pause with my hand on the front doorknob.

*The only way to have the life I want is to go after it. I've got this.*

Pep-talk complete, I saunter outside.

Gideon glances my way. He splits a few more logs, then buries the ax in the stump and grabs his T-shirt to wipe the sweat from his brow.

God, he's even hotter up close. I don't think there's an ounce of fat on him. Rivulets of sweat trickle over every delicious ridge, heading down toward that intriguing line of dark hair that disappears beneath his jeans. His arms are thick with muscle and half a dozen scars pepper his skin. It's the body of a warrior. A man who puts himself in the line of danger for others. People like me. Like my dad.

My heart drops to my toes and bounces back in a rush that makes me dizzy.

*Oh no.* I think I'm in love with Gideon Blake.

"Amber?"

How did that happen? Yes, I know I'm attracted to him, but doesn't it take longer to fall in love? Even cartoon princesses take longer, right?

"Is that water for me?"

Could it really be love if it's only been a day?

Gideon gently removes the water bottle from my grip. "Hey. You okay?" His concerned eyes soften when I meet his gaze. "There she is."

"I..." Might be in love with you. Not fair, Universe. Not. Fair. "Um... water." I wave vaguely at the bottle he's already opened and chugged a third of.

His lips twitch. "Tried to let you sleep. I know you needed it."

From the start, he's taken care of me. Like he's being paid to do. "I wish it was more than that."

"More than what?"

I cover my face with my hands, then cringe because one is cold and wet from holding the water bottle. Gah. What am I doing out here? I spin back toward the house, wiping my face dry.

Gideon snags my arm and pulls me to a stop. "What's going on in that pretty head of yours, honey?" He pulls me around to face him and cups my cheek.

The warm comfort of that touch hurts. I thought I could waltz out here and boldly tell him that I wanted him. I hoped he'd see me as a woman who is on the cusp of coming into her own, strong enough to stand up to the forces that would try to knock her down. Instead, I tripped over my heart and fell on my face.

I had it all wrong. The Universe was definitely flipping me off.

Gideon's fingers thread through my hair, pulling it free from the messy bun I keep it in.

I sigh at the touch and realize I've closed my eyes. When I open them, all I can see is his concern.

He tucks a strand of hair behind my ear. "Talk to me, Amber."

I can't. I can't separate the maelstrom of emotions swirling inside. Instead, I go up on my toes and kiss him again. It's probably the worst thing I could do, but what the hell? I can flip off the Universe too.

# CHAPTER SEVEN
## *Gideon*

Confusion, frustration, awe, desire... it's all there on Amber's pretty face. It probably matches my own. I've been out here since dawn obliterating logs because I couldn't hold her in my arms a second more without rolling her underneath me and feasting on that delectable body.

I woke flat on my back on the couch, with Amber draped over my chest. My favorite shirt was warm from her skin and silky soft beneath my hand. I stroked a hand down her back, still half asleep until my hand met bare skin. The shirt had ridden up, and I suddenly had a palm full of her plump ass. My morn-ing wood turned into a full hard-on so fast my head swam from blood loss.

I shifted out from under her as gently as I could and fled like a coward.

Jesus, look at us. Dancing around each other, drawn together like magnets, and trying to fight the pull.

I set the water down and draw her closer. Her beautiful hair entices me, and I spear my fingers into it, gently working it from the rubber band until the silky length flows free. Her eyes slide close and she leans into my touch. The world around us falls away until there is only the two of us in this moment.

When her eyes open, the honey brown color is so rich and deep that it catches my breath. I tuck a strand behind her ear, wanting to see more.

She still hasn't spoken. "Talk to me, Amber."

Her lips part and her minty breath washes over me, then her mouth is on mine.

Why was I fighting this? Yes, it breaks every one of my carefully crafted rules. We're at different points in our lives. Her father's a client. Despite all of that, she's mine. She was made for me. I don't know how I know, only that I've never been surer of anything in my life. This is real.

I palm her ass and lift her up. Her legs go around my waist and my dick pushes against her core. Too many clothes. I need her naked and underneath me. Now.

"Amber." My voice rasps out low and rough. Can she hear how much I want her? I don't want there to be any doubt. Not this time. I start for the cabin. The second she says she wants me, I want to strip her clothes off and sink inside that hot pussy. "Honey, I'm sorry that I pushed you away last night. I was trying to protect you."

"I know," she says softly. She places a kiss at the base of my throat.

Shit. I might not make it inside with her. I want that mouth all over me. I'm so hard, I'm leaking in my jeans. "I'm—"

Bullets slam into the side of the cabin six inches to my left. I dive for the porch, covering her with my body. A dozen shots ring out, hitting above us, and chips of wood shower down on our heads. I cover her as best I can. Whoever is firing is not trying to hit us at least.

I scan the surroundings and spot a glint of metal twenty yards away at the edge of the tree line. We're at the corner of the cabin, partially hidden from view by a flowering bush, but it won't give us any protection if these assholes get impatient.

"Bring her out and we won't kill you," a nasally male voice calls.

Very impatient.

I pull Amber behind the bush so we're completely hidden and remove my Sig Sauer from the holster at the small of my back.

"What are we going to do?" Amber whispers. She's gripping my arm so tight that I can feel the tremor roll through her.

There's no way we can get to either the truck or the front door of the cabin from here. Even the nearest window is too exposed. Plus, I locked it last night. The only way to get it open is to break the glass and risk injuring her.

Another round of bullets hits the cabin.

"The next shots are aimed at you," the man yells.

Amber sucks in a breath.

"They won't shoot us. They wouldn't risk hitting you when they can't see exactly where you are." It's a pretty thick and wide bush. So full that it's set away from the porch a good ten or eleven inches to allow for growth. I lean over the edge of the porch, hoping for a hiding spot. Even better, there's a crawlspace underneath the cabin.

I press a fast kiss to Amber's lips. "When I say go, jump down there and slide under the cabin. Try to stay in line with the bush and go all the way the other side."

"What are you going to do?"

"I'm going to buy you a couple minutes and disguise any noise by shooting back. I'll be right behind you. As soon as we're on the other side, we'll run for the woods. Got it?"

She nods. Her face is pale, but the set of her chin tells me that she's ready. "You can do this. I'm getting you out of here, honey. Then we'll finish what we started."

Her eyes mist and a tiny smile touches her mouth. She nods.

"Get ready."

Amber scrambles to the edge of the porch. As soon as she's in place, I whisper, "Go!"

She drops down behind the bush and scrambles under the cabin. At the same time, I lean out far enough to lay down cover fire. I'm limited to the sixteen rounds in my weapon and another fifteen in my second clip. It needs to be enough.

After half a dozen shots, I holster my weapon and follow her down.

"There are *spiders*," she hisses from the darkness. "You didn't say anything about spiders, Gideon Blake." Her curvy ass is ahead of me, crawling toward the light on the other side.

Jesus, I love this woman.

The thought closes my throat, but I press on. There'll be time to examine that later.

We make it to the edge of the cabin. I can hear the man yelling from the other side. The woods are ten yards away from here. I watch for a few precious seconds, but nothing moves within. If we can make it to the trees unseen, we can wait them out and hopefully return for the truck. I don't want my woman out here without shelter any longer than necessary.

I draw my weapon once more. "Get ready to run. Head that way." I point at an angle that will keep the cabin directly between us and her kidnappers. So long as they're not fanning out yet, we have a chance. "Run as fast as you can. Once you get inside the woods, stop. We don't want to make any noise."

Amber nods.

"Go!"

She crawls out from under the cabin and runs. I emerge behind her, weapon ready to protect her. We make it to the trees without incident.

It's almost too easy.

# CHAPTER EIGHT
## *Amber*

**M**y heart is pounding so loud, I'm sure the kidnappers can hear it. The only thing keeping me together is Gideon. He guides me quietly through the woods until the cabin is no longer in sight.

I can't hear the men anymore and it terrifies me. There's something to be said for knowing exactly where your enemy is. Not knowing is far, far worse. Every sound makes me jump.

Gideon stops a few minutes later. I sag against a tree and lean over, desperately dragging air into my lungs. Panic is choking me and I can't breathe.

His warm hand strokes my back. "Easy," he murmurs. "You're safe."

His touch soothes me, and the panic slowly recedes. "How did they find us?"

"Derek told me last night that news outlets were playing video footage of the fight at your apartment yesterday. I'm willing to bet someone at the super-store recognized you. They're probably getting their fifteen minutes of fame and leading these assholes right to us as a result."

"But how could they find us here? We're in the middle of nowhere."

"You'd be amazed at what money can do, senorita," a man says in a thick, His-panic accent.

Gideon backs me against the tree and stands in front of me, literally shielding me with his body. His gun is aimed at the man. "You don't speak to her."

I get a glimpse of the man as Gideon shifts to keep him in sight. He's close to my height, with thinning black hair and a rotund stature. His black eyes flick to me and I suppress a shudder. They're soulless.

The man clicks his tongue. "You will find I can do whatever I want."

"If that were true, Dominguez, you wouldn't need to terrorize a woman to reach your goal."

The man laughs. "You know who I am. Would it surprise you that I know who you are also, Gideon Blake? Former Delta Forces, former green beret, former army grunt." His lips twist in a smile. "Former bodyguard to Senorita Mayfield."

Gideon's shoulders flex.

That's when I see a bunch of Hispanic men step out of the woods, fanning around us with their weapons drawn.

In the distance, there's a *whump-whump-whump* sound. It seems to be getting closer.

"That sounds like my helicopter," Dominguez says cheerfully. "Time to decide, Blake. Do you hand her over to us or do you die while we take her from you?"

"No!" The word rips out of my throat. I can't go with them. I know they'll kill me when they get what they want from my father. But I'll never survive if they kill Gideon.

"It's okay, honey," he whispers. His left hand finds my hip, holding me still.

How can it possibly be okay? He's standing in front of me, shirtless, shielding me with his body while half a dozen men are waiting to kill him, and eventually me. I wrap my arms around him from behind. "Please don't hurt him."

Dominguez rubs his hands together. "How sweet. She cares for you, Blake. Do you think she would trade for your life?"

"Not if she's smart," Gideon replies.

What's that supposed to mean?

The sound of a gun cocking makes me jump. One of the men to our left levels a revolver at us.

"Last chance, senorita."

Gideon squeezes my hip *hard*.

Gunfire erupts around us.

A scream tears loose from my lips. I expect to see Gideon collapse and to feel the pain of a bullet. Instead, the men around us jerk and fall to the forest floor.

*Bam! Bam! Bam!*

Dominguez twitches, pools of red staining his white shirt. He smiles at Gideon, then drops to his knees. A second later, he pitches face first to the ground.

Silence.

I uncover my ears, gasping for breath. I hadn't even realized that I'd covered them. My gaze snags on Gideon's right hand. His gun is aimed where Dominguez once stood.

"Asshole," Gideon mutters, holstering his gun.

Or maybe he said it normal. Everything sounds far away.

He turns to me and cups my cheeks. "Are you okay?"

"We're not dead."

His grin lights up his face. "No, we're not dead."

"Well you're fucking lucky that I found you," another man gripes. He stomps up and slaps a tattooed hand on Gideon's shoulder. "You're welcome."

Gideon laughs and leans into a bro hug. They pound each other on the back. "Good to see you, Derek."

So this is his business partner. The man is an inch shorter than Gideon. He has two full sleeves by the looks of it, the tattoos going all the way to his hands. I glimpse faces hidden in the ink, but can't make them out.

Gideon introduces us, and then the three other men Derek brought with him: Keane, Sol, and Lincoln. They make up the rest of Citadel Securities.

"If your ugly mugs are here, who's minding the store?" Gideon asks.

It's Keane that groans. "Winter. Better pray the bar is still there when we get back."

Derek rolls his eyes. "She's more capable of running it than you, asshole." To Gideon, he says, "The Senator texted twenty minutes ago. The vote is beginning now."

"Better let him know the threat is over."

Derek nods. "Way to bag Dominguez. I think that makes it twelve to ten."

"Nice try. Dominguez today and Ramirez last month. We're tied."

Derek winks at me. "Kill The Cartel is no fun if you can't cheat."

Gideon pulls me into his arms. "Get out of here. I'll bring her back."

Derek's gaze slides back and forth between us. "Taking the long route, I presume?"

"It might take a few days."

Derek nods. He reaches out to cup my shoulder and give it a gentle squeeze. "Welcome to the family." Then he whistles, and the three other men melt back into the trees behind him.

Gideon presses his lips to my temple.

"Is it over?" I'm afraid to hope.

"It's over. By the time we get back to the cabin, your father should know you're safe. He can vote however he chooses."

"How did Derek find us?"

Gideon taps his watch. "Tracker. It's only traceable to us. Knowing Derek, he monitored the news all night. The moment someone said they'd seen us, he would have rounded up the guys to come charging to the rescue."

"Thank god."

"Yeah, except I'm never going to hear the end of it." Gideon grins despite his grumbling. "Come on, honey. Let's grab our stuff and get out of here."

He takes my hand, leading me back toward the cabin. I bite my bottom lip as we walk, afraid to say what's on my mind.

*The only way to have the life I want is to go after it.*

The last hour has shown me there's one thing I want more than anything. Even more than my degree. I swallow, pull up my courage, and ask, "What happens after that?"

Gideon stops walking and faces me. "What do you want to happen?"

"I want to make love to you, Gideon. And then I want to be with you."

He steps closer. "No going back to Texas?"

"No."

"For how long, honey? How long do you want me?"

I wind my arms around his neck. "For as long as you'll give me. Hopefully, forever."

A slow smile spreads across his face, lighting up his eyes. "I'm all yours."

# CHAPTER NINE
## *Gideon*

As nice as this cabin was, I'm not going to make love to my woman in a place with bad memories.

We pack up our few belongings, then climb into my truck, which has a couple new holes courtesy of the Dominguez cartel, and leave Mississippi behind.

It's late afternoon when we arrive at the plantation in Louisiana. A large, wrought-iron gate bars entry. I dig the remote out of my glove box to open it, then pull onto an oak lined drive.

"What is this place?" Amber leans forward, trying to take in her surroundings. An enormous antebellum mansion lies ahead. Scaffolding is set up around the second-story balcony and the front doors are still boarded over. We turn right at the end of the drive and stop by what used to be the carriage house. It's fully restored and now boasts four bedrooms, four baths, and its own kitchen.

"This is Belle Grove. Sol bought it a decade ago. He said it called to him and knew it was meant to be his. Since we left the service, we've all spent weekends here helping with the restoration." I turn off the truck and go around to her side to help her down. "Now that the carriage house is finished, we stay here whenever we're out this way."

I guide her inside, and the catch of her breath makes me smile. We restored as much as we could, and Sol had a designer in to meld the mid-nineteenth century with modern features.

"It's gorgeous."

"Absolutely." I'm not looking at the house. Amber is all I can see. I reach for her and gently tug her hair out of the bun until it falls around her shoulders. I want to see it spread out on my pillow.

Right now.

I lift her in my arms and throw her over my shoulder, taking the stairs two at a time.

She squeals. "Put me down!"

I slap her ass. "No."

She gasps, and I swear it's half pleasure. Did my girl like that?

She leans down and spanks my ass. "Yes!"

I laugh and run the rest of the way to the bedroom I use when I'm here. I toss her on the bed, then come down over her until we're pressed together.

"Did you mean it, honey?"

"Yes. I wanted you to put me down."

I tug her lower lip between my teeth, then lick it. "Do you want me forever?"

Her face softens. "And forever after that."

My heart soars. I sit up and rip my shirt off, tossing it behind me. Amber's hands are on my chest but she's getting ahead of herself. "Not yet. Strip."

She grins and reaches for her shirt.

Too slow. I slide my hands under her shirt and pull it over her head. It flies back to land somewhere near mine. I strip the rest of her clothes off then move her into the center of the bed.

"Off," she says, tugging at my belt loop.

I kick off my boots, then drop the rest of my clothes and climb back over her. Nothing has ever felt as good as being skin to skin with this woman. Her hard nipples scrape against my chest and my dick slides between her wet folds. "Shit, honey." I flex my hips and slide back through. I am not going to last unless I slow this down. But first...

"I'm clean. I've never been with any-one without a condom."

Her cheeks flush. "I... uh... am too."

Because she's a virgin? I brush her hair from her face and press a soft kiss to her lips. It soon grows heated and she moans. I kiss my way down her neck, letting my hands fill with every gorgeous curve. Her tits fill my hands perfectly, her nipples hard points against my palms. I take one in my mouth, then the other, suckling her until she's panting.

My hand slides through the wetness between her legs. "You're soaked, honey. Can't wait to feel you." But first, I need to taste that pussy.

I move down between her thighs, hooking her legs over my shoulders and swipe my tongue through her folds. Holy fuck. I've gone to heaven. "Could do this forever," I murmur against her folds. She is the most delicious meal I've ever had. I lick and suck and kiss her until she's crying out my name, her hips riding my face. Beautiful. One more hard lick is all it takes to push her over the edge. She comes hard for me. So sweet.

Before she's completely recovered, I crawl back up her body and position my cock at her entrance. I think it's her first time, but she's still lost in pleasure and I don't want to draw attention to it. She's loose and relaxed right now. If she tenses, it will hurt more. I don't want her first memory of sex to be one of pain.

"Ready?" I ask.

She nods. "Please."

I notch my head at her entrance and push in until I feel resistance. My grin is feral at the confirmation she's a virgin. I'm going to be her first. Her only. "You're mine, Amber. Now. *Always*."

She nods.

I lean forward and capture her lips in a hard kiss, then push through the barrier and claim her.

She gasps against my mouth.

"Shhh. It's okay."

Amber winds her arms around my neck and holds tight. Less than a minute later, she kisses me. "Please, Gideon. More."

I withdraw and give a shallow thrust, sliding through her wet heat. She's so tight, I'm about to come. "Jesus, you feel incredible."

"You too."

I push into her, again and again, until her hips rise to meet my thrusts. "Good girl."

She shivers at the compliment.

Damn this woman is perfect. I slide my hand between us and rub her clit, pushing her higher and higher. Her inner muscles grip me hard. The pleasure is overwhelming.

Before I can pull out, she wraps her legs around my hips and anchors me to her as she begins to come.

"Honey..."

Amber kisses me. "I love you, Gideon."

Her words take me straight over the edge into the longest, hardest orgasm I've ever had. I collapse beside her and pull her against me. "I love you too, honey. I love you too."

# EPILOGUE
## Amber

*Two Months Later*

I save the document I've been working on for weeks, then print it. I can't believe it's finally done. The door to the small office bangs open just as I'm reaching for the printer and Derek strolls in.

"One of these days you and your boyfriend are going to have to find your own damn office and stop using mine."

"But yours is more comfortable when we—"

He holds up a tattooed hand. "Stop. Don't say it. If you were about to say when you two have sex, I'm going to burn every piece of furniture in here."

I laugh. "I was going to say 'when we have a business meeting to talk about the expansion.'"

He scowls as if he doesn't quite believe me. What he doesn't know won't hurt him, right?

I grab the papers from the printer. "Is he out there?"

Derek grunts and shoos me out of his space. I walk out into the hall and then into the Double Tap Bar. It's a Friday night, and the place is packed with a mix of tourists and locals. I love it here.

When we returned to New Orleans a few days after the Senate vote, Gideon and my father contacted my school and convinced them to let me take my final exams. I was surprised that my father helped make the arrangements.

After the kidnapping incident, I worried that my parents would double down on their overprotectiveness. I was ready to fight them for the life I wanted.

My father was so grateful that I was safe, he didn't even bat an eye to learn that Gideon and I are dating. He said the incident made him realize how short life can be and he wouldn't hold me back any longer. My mom is a little more of a work in progress, but with dad on my side, she's coming around.

I passed my final exams and graduated with a business degree last month. Since then, I've talked with the guys about smart ways to expand. That's what I've just finished: the business plan.

I find Gideon behind the antique bar that takes up an entire wall. Wood tables cover a black and white checkered floor. Brass accents add a bit of shine and the French doors are open to let in the autumn breeze.

Gideon moves over to kiss my temple and nods toward the end of the bar. Winter, one of the main waitresses is squared off with Keane, her arms crossed over her chest. The sexual tension between these two is enough to set off the fire alarm, but Keane always backs down for some reason. Gideon won't tell me why, and I think it must have something to do with their service days.

Keane stares at Winter, then slowly shakes his head.

She throws her hands in the air. "Fine. You don't have to go. I'll find someone else." She sounds more resigned than mad.

I know she likes him. Actually, I think everyone but Keane knows that she likes him.

Winter walks away, back straight, grabs a glass from the bar, and takes it to a table full of young men. Keane stiffens.

Just when I think he'll finally follow, he turns away.

I shake my head.

Gideon chuckles. "They'll work it out. He won't be able to see her around other men much longer."

"How do you know?"

"Because I can't stand seeing other men fawning over you. You're mine."

I smile and kiss him. "I am."

He traces my lower lip with his finger. "That your business plan?"

"Yes. It's ready."

"Good. Let's go home and study it for a long, long time."

I laugh when he wraps his arms around me. "Aren't we leaving for Montana tomorrow?"

His sister Harmony and Caleb are getting married. Something that Gideon is still working through. When Caleb agreed to return to White Falls to protect Harmony from a stalker, the feelings he'd been harboring for her quickly came to the surface. Harmony had pined for him just as long, unbeknownst to Gideon, and they fell in love. Gideon loves them both. He knows no one will protect Harmony as well as Caleb, but sometimes he struggles to see his sister as an adult who's old enough to start her own family. That will change when he walks her down the aisle.

Gideon takes my hand and draws me toward the stairs. We live in one of the apartments above. "If we miss their wedding, they'll just have to come to ours."

I stumble to a stop. "What?"

He brings my hand to his lips, pressing a kiss over my ring finger. "You didn't think I'd let you get away, did you? I promised you forever, honey, and I'm a man of my word."

"Are you asking me or telling me?"

"Which one will make you say yes?"

He laughs before I can answer, then pulls me up the stairs. When he opens the door to our apartment, I see rose petals scattered everywhere. There's a black tablecloth on the dining table, and in the center is a blue velvet box.

"Marry me, Amber. Be mine forever."

I spin in his arms and kiss him. "Yes!"

He chuckles against my mouth. "Good, because you're mine, honey. Only mine."

I hope you enjoyed Gideon and Amber's story. Turn the page to read another story in the Citadel Securities connected world – An ex-soldier driving across country to take a new job makes a wrong turn and finds the right kind of love.

# Lost For You

*By Ash Henry*

# Chapter One
## *Everett*

*Where the hell am I?*

I rub my right eye with my palm and blink against the setting sun. Montana, but where? This sure as fuck isn't the main highway that I was on. Or is it? God damn, if I paid attention to my surroundings like this in Force Recon, I would have gotten killed on the first day.

I rub the muscles in my neck that are aching and look for a decent road sign. Big, beautiful mountains surround me, their peaks already snowy even though it's the end of September. I roll down the window to get a blast of cold autumn air. It clears my head a little, and right after, I see a sign for White Falls. Beyond that, a county road number. Definitely off course. But maybe that's not a bad thing. I could turn around and go back until I hook up with Highway 2, but I can't remember the last sign I saw for food, and right now, coffee seems like a pretty damn good idea. I can get a decent meal and then decide if I push on or if I should just stop for the night.

White Falls turns out to be a quaint small town. The kind you'd find in a Christmas movie where Main Street is packed with shops, a diner, and even a movie theater. There's even a town square at the end with an old, wrought iron clock and a little park. It's... nice. The kind you'd want to raise a family in. Not that I have any plans for that shit.

I park the truck in front of the diner and run my hand through my hair. Since I left the military three months ago, I've been lost. I'm only taking this security job in Seattle to give myself something to do. It's not like I want to move there. But I can't keep staring at the fucking walls, asking myself what I'm doing. Who I am. I'm hoping the change of location will give me a purpose. If it doesn't, I don't know what the fuck I'm going to do. Go bat shit crazy probably. God help the people around me.

I shove out of the truck, sick of my maudlin thoughts, and kick the door closed. Coffee. Food. In that order. Then I can decide what's next. One foot in front of the other.

The diner is clean and bright, with a couple dozen tables and dark blue booths, plus a counter with stools. I see why the place is packed. It smells heavenly. Like burgers, and sandwiches, and Thanksgiving dinner.

"Pick a seat and we'll be right there," an older waitress calls to me.

I slide into a booth in back where I can clock the exits and catalog the people around me. It's habit, but I'm off my game tonight because I completely miss the gorgeous woman coming toward me until she's standing at my table.

"Hey. Welcome to Gravy Lane," she says in the sweetest voice I've ever heard and hands me a menu.

"Wh-what's your name?" I stutter out like a stupefied teen boy. But god, can you blame me? Her long, honey blonde hair makes me want to wrap my fist around it while I pull her mouth to mine for a hungry kiss on those plush pink lips. Would those baby blue eyes go darker with desire?

"Uh, what?"

I shake my head to clear the instant fog of lust and only manage to make myself slightly more intelligent, because there's a lot less blood in my brain right now. I've got an erection from the sound of her voice. That's never happened be-fore.

Before I can force an apology out for staring at her, the corner of her mouth quirks up.

"Lacey. My name is Lacey." She waves at her black button up dress. "I for-got my name tag at home this morn-ing. Since everyone here knows me, you caught me by surprise."

I'm not an animal, so I don't stare at her breasts when she just waved her hand at them, but that doesn't mean that I don't notice how that dress hugs every delectable curve. I love that she's not stick thin. I work meticulously to keep my body in top shape for any situa-tion. My muscles are hard. When I pull a woman close, I want to feel her softness against me. Not that I can remember the last time I experienced that.

Lacey looks at me expectantly, and it's clear I missed a question.

I raise my brows.

Her throaty laughter and the dimples in her cheeks make my cock so hard it hurts. God damn, it's been too long since I got laid. But a quickie with a waitress while passing through her small town isn't appealing. Everything about this woman says she's worth much more than a one-nighter.

I surreptitiously adjust myself as she repeats her question about a drink.

"Coffee please. Black is fine."

"Sure thing. Take your time with that menu. Everything is really good here."

Our eyes meet, and heat flickers in my stomach. "Everything?"

"You won't be disappointed." Her cheeks turn pink as soon as the words are out of her mouth. "Let me get that coffee."

I catch her wrist as she spins away, holding her gently. Her skin is like satin beneath my fingers. "My name is

Everett." I don't know why I tell her that. It's not like there will ever be anything between us. I just... I'm not ready for her to leave yet. There's something about her. A pull I've never felt before.

She flashes that sweet smile at me, and her shoulders relax the tiniest bit. Like she's relieved that the innocent flirtation didn't put me off. "Nice to meet you, Everett. Think about what you want. I'll be right back with your coffee."

Lacey steps away, and I reluctantly release her.

Think about what I want. I've been doing that for three months and I still don't have an answer. One thing I do know. Even if I wanted Lacey, she's not for me. I don't live here and I've got at least a decade on her. I've seen things that would give her nightmares, while she radiates an innocence I haven't felt since long before I entered the military.

What do I want? Only things that I can't have. Nothing new there.

# CHAPTER TWO

## Lacey

"You okay, hon?" Lorraine, the other waitress here at Gravy Lane, asks me. "You're looking a bit pink." Her eyes twinkle as she tucks a stray length of graying hair into her bun, because she knows why I'm flustered.

Not many men who look like *that* pass through White Falls. Sure, we have our share of handsome guys, and some who only look good on the outside, but none of them radiate an intensity like Everett.

"I'm fine." I glance back at his table to find him staring at me instead of his menu. My flush deepens, but I can't help smiling at him. He made me feel at ease after I became flustered. It says something about a man. He could have shrugged it off, ignored me, or even told me to leave. Instead, he held my wrist so that I would stay.

Lorraine chuckles. "Smitten, I'd say. I don't think I've seen you go out with anyone since you moved here. Which was what... six months ago?"

I nod and grab a clean mug to fill with coffee. I quit college to move to a tiny town that only grows when babies are born. But I'd do it again tomorrow if Henry needed me. "I've never been good around guys. They usually want someone... different."

"You mean thinner? Hon, not all men like lollipops when it comes to their candy. I think you've been around too many *boys*."

"Maybe." The boys I knew in high school and college were more interested in my thin friends than me. Since moving to White Falls, I haven't had time to think about dating. Despite the occasional bit of insecurity over my curves, sometime in the last six months, I realized that while I might not be supermodel material, most days I like who I am and what I look like. My limited experience insists that a gorgeous guy like Everett wouldn't look twice at me, but what if Lorraine is right?

"Lacey, let me tell you something your mamma should have been telling you since you could talk. You're beautiful, inside and out. Any man who can't see that isn't worth your time. That man over there staring at you? I think he *sees* you. Now get over there and lay on that charm."

My heart thumps hard when I feel those intense eyes on me. "It's not like he's staying, Lorraine. He said he's just passing through."

"Then go practice for the man who stays." She gives me a little shove and I work not to spill his coffee as I cross the diner.

The bell above the door jingles, and a gust of cold autumn air swirls through the diner when a group of five cowboys saunter in. I spot Colby Tucker in the lead and squash down a groan. Of all the times for him to show up. Why couldn't he have waited an hour until after Everett was on his way? Avoiding his dark gaze, I weave through tables and place the coffee on Everett's table.

Charm. I can do this. I paste a smile on my face. "Decide what you wanted?"

"Look at me, Lacey."

His gruff, commanding voice sends a shiver through me. Does he use that voice all the time? An image sneaks into my brain of him hovering over me, pressing me into the mattress while holding my hands above my head, and commanding me to come. My belly tightens and I press my thighs together against the needy pulse the fantasy gives me.

I meet his eyes. In the fluorescent light of the diner, they look gray, like gunmetal. His dark hair is longer on top than the sides, but it's clear he hasn't had it cut in a while. A couple days of beard growth covers his strong jaw and frame a firm, kissable mouth. His shoulders a wonderfully broad and the gray henley he's wearing conforms to the muscles in his arms.

"Lacey."

I realize my gaze has wandered and lock eyes with him. "Yes?"

A faint smile teases the left corner of his mouth. He gives a chin lift toward the cowboys who've settled at the table in the center of the diner, where everyone can hear their raucous behavior. "They going to be a problem for you?"

"Uh... no." Not as long as Tucker keeps his mouth shut. "Besides, my shift is over soon."

He looks at the chunky black watch on his wrist. "It's just after four. You only work the lunch shift?"

"I have things to take care of in the evenings."

Everett sits forward, moving the menu aside. "Like what?"

"Hey Lacey! Get your big ass over here," Tucker yells over the clamor of the other diners, purposely letting his voice carry. "We're thirsty."

I grit my teeth and look over my shoulder. Tucker trains his tight smile and narrowed eyes on me. He knows he's being an ass in front of everyone. He doesn't care so long as it embarrasses me. Another case of a nasty personality behind good looks.

"I got them, Lacey. Finish with your other customers," Lorraine says as she skirts past.

I nod, feeling the heat creep up my face. When I turn back to Everett, he's half out of the booth, looking pissed.

"It's okay." His shoulders are like granite beneath my hands as I try to push him back toward his seat. "They're just rude idiots."

Everett grips my hips, trying to move me aside. "He can't talk to you like that."

I push back. "Please don't make a scene. I can't lose this job."

He snarls something under his breath, sitting down hard. The movement pulls me off balance and I pitch forward into the booth, flailing for purchase. Everett tries to steady me and I grab the back of the booth over his head, almost tumbling into his lap. He smells so good up close. I suck in another breath. One laced with pine and a hint of citrus.

Clean and manly. Everett's warm breath gusts over my neck, making my skin prickle with awareness. The image of sitting in his lap, nuzzling his neck while I grind against the hard bulge in his jeans, fills my head and I nearly moan when my core floods in response.

"Hmm." Everett's throaty sound is almost a rumble of pleasure and his hands flex on my hips, pulling me closer.

I glance down to see what he's looking at and... oh god. My boobs are almost smooshed in his face, and half the town is here to witness it.

He looks up with heated gray eyes. "I should order coffee more often."

He keeps hold of me until I'm steady on my feet, his thumb rubbing a circle on my hip. Part of me wants to lean into his touch, but the sheer mortification from the last few minutes is stronger. Even if I never see Everett again, I know Tucker will tease me about this for months. He'll make sure every-one knows about the clumsy waitress who tackled a poor restaurant patron.

A person can't really die of embar-rassment, right? Desperate for a few minutes to collect myself, I reply with a cringey: "Welcome to White Falls!" Then I dash for the kitchen.

# Chapter Three
## *Everett*

Lacey keeps her distance from the loudmouth motherfucker who insulted her, and he's settled down some with his friends. Good for him, since I was seconds away from ramming my fist in his face. He tracks her every time she walks by to help a customer, and it doesn't take a genius to realize that he wants her. Fucker has a bad way of showing it.

I don't know why I care, but I do. She brings out a protective instinct in me that's primal. Since the second I saw Lacey's sweet smile, I wanted it all for myself. The less she turns it on that asshole, the better. He needs a lesson on how to treat a woman. Too bad I won't be here long enough to do the job myself.

I should finish the burger and fries Lacey brought me a few minutes ago and get back on the road. Put in a few more hours of driving. Maybe find a motel in Idaho and make Seattle tomorrow. But fuck, I can't go. Not yet.

I tell myself that it's because I'm too tired and know I should rest. I've pushed hard to get across the country. Not because I'm in a hurry. There's just nothing back in Philly for me anymore. There's nothing for me anywhere.

Since I discharged, there's a restlessness inside me. An emptiness like a growing void of darkness reaching into every corner of my soul. Fucking overly dramatic, but true. It grows by the day, reminding me with every breath that I have no purpose. No one *needs* me anymore.

Back in my unit, we were in some pretty fucked up situations. We relied on each other to make it through. They were my brothers for years. The only family I had. Now, there's no one. Most of the guys are still deployed, and the ones that aren't... it's hard to come back to everyday life. We all deal with it in different ways. For me, at first I cut myself off from that life, those men, entirely. Now I just don't know what to say. To them or to myself.

"Hey there, Everett. Can I get you anything else?" Lacey returns, breaking me out of my fucking depressive thoughts. She's so lovely, with her golden hair and generous curves. Like a ray of sunshine aimed right at me.

"How about a recommendation? I need to stop for the night. Is there a motel around here?"

She lights up at that. Does she feel this connection like I do? Does she hope I'll stay a little longer?

"There's a motel at the edge of town."

She points in that direction with a bright pink painted nail. They're kept short, and I can't help but notice how soft her hands look. How would they feel on my skin? Wrapped around my cock? The thought makes my dick hard all over again.

"Maybe you could come by the diner for breakfast? Before you leave." She glances at me from under her lashes and it's the sexiest look I've ever seen. Sweetness and pure temptation.

"Will you be working tomorrow?"

"I'll be in by eight a.m. Once..." She shakes her head a little. "Anyway, yes. I will. Maybe I will see you?" She presses her lips together and watches me.

Is that I hope I see on her face? Maybe it's the loneliness or just plain attraction, but I want it to be. I want to see Lacey again. Nothing will come of it. I know that. It doesn't stop me from promising to be here.

"So um... where are you headed?"

Jesus, I want to kiss her. Haul her into my lap right here and find out how those lips taste. It's madness because I've only known her for forty-five minutes. Less than an hour of watching the smile she gives her customers as she chats and laughs with them and holding the door for an elderly couple. The steel in her spine as she walks past that group of idiot cowboys. Forty-five minutes of cataloging her every move. Which is long enough, apparently, with the way my heart is thumping in my chest. I have to clear my throat to reply. "Seattle. Got a job starting up in a week."

Her shoulders slump. "I hear it's beautiful out there. Do you have family waiting for you?"

It takes every bit of restraint I possess not to touch her. I want to take her hand in mine and feel the warmth of her palm. I'm losing it over this woman, and I have no idea why. "No. No family. I... don't have one." Don't know why I tell her that. I don't tell *anyone* that.

"That must be hard." She edges closer. "I don't know what brought you here, Everett, but I'm glad you stopped."

"Me too." I give in and catch her wrist again.

Her breath catches, and her eyes dilate at the touch. She turns her hand and our fingers lace together. "Everett..."

"It's almost 4:30, Lacey," the older waitress calls.

Lacey slips her hand from mine and clenches it into a fist. "My shift is over. Is there anything else I can get you?"

*All the time I can get with you.* I don't say that. That's creeper talk even to my tired brain. "Breakfast tomorrow?"

"I'll be here."

"Looking forward to it." I pay my bill with a generous tip, then leave her to finish up. I'm halfway out the door when I hear that obnoxious cowboy again.

"Looks like your lover left without you, Lacey. How about you spend time with a real man?"

"Let me know when you find one, Colby Tucker," she snaps as she strides past, head held high.

His friends laugh, but the look he gives Lacey is one I'm familiar with. She wounded his pride in front of half of this small town. It's a slight he has no problem dealing out but can't take, and the clenching of his fist and narrowed eyes promise retribution.

Instead of heading for my truck, I find a spot where I can see both the front and side doors of the diner and wait. Lacey might not be my woman, but there's no fucking way I'll allow her to get hurt while I'm here.

Five minutes later, she comes out the side door into the alley between the buildings, bundled up in a bright pink coat and scarf. The temperature has dropped at least fifteen degrees as the sun sets on this mountain town. I straighten up from the wall of the building next door. She sees me just as the front door of the diner opens and Tucker and his friends spill out.

The smile he gives Lacey is nasty with dark promise. He stalks towards her. "Where you going, Lacey? Don't you want that date?"

His friends snicker and follow, eagerness in every line of their bodies as they wait to see what happens.

Lacey's spine goes stiff. "Not with you, Tucker. How many times do I have to say it?"

"I think I can change your mind." He crowds her back into the growing shadows between buildings, his friends close behind.

I stride toward them. Looks like I can teach him some manners after all. The thought makes me smile.

# CHAPTER FOUR
## *Lacey*

"**W**hy the hell would I want to go out with you when you just called me fat in front of half the town, Tucker? What kind of women have you dated in the past that fall at your feet when you insult them?" I don't have time to deal with him. I'm already running late to relieve Alice and I don't want her to have to wait for me.

I try to push past him, but he crowds me back against the wall of the restaurant and I sense his friends closing in. Surrounding us until they've blocked the exit to the alley.

Tucker's cologne washes over me, something masculine, citrusy, and popular, since all his friends wear it too. I'd complain, but they're masking the scent of the alley, which smells like old, wet garbage thanks to the rain we had earlier. "I wouldn't have to insult you if you quit turning me down."

My jaw really drops this time. "What kind of dumb logic is that?" Is he for real? "Even if I liked you, which I don't, I can't go out with you. Henry needs me."

Shoving at Tucker's chest only moves him back a step. With his sandy blond hair, green eyes, and hard body, Colby Tucker would be jaw-dropping if it weren't for his personality. He's a crude bully, more interested in showing off to his friends than how someone else might feel. "Move. Now."

"Why would I do that when I finally have your attention?" He cages me in against the brick wall, hands on either side of my head.

Swallowing hard, I straighten my back and clench my hands to stop them from shaking as I realize my predicament. I shouldn't have goaded him. I embarrassed him in public, and the hard glint in his eyes says I'm going to pay for it. My heart starts to pound. I'm trapped in an alley that's growing darker by the minute, in a town that has zero nightlife. Thoughts of what could happen flash through my head, making my stomach roll.

"You sure seemed to have time for that guy you were flirting with a few minutes ago. You gonna sneak out on your grandpa to spread your legs for him, Lacey? Better a stranger to fuck than someone you know?"

He did not just say that. Fury at the insult burns through my fear. I slap him as hard as I can and shove him back, but don't make it a step before Tucker latches onto my arm and yanks me against him. "Get off me!" Balling my fists, I aim for anything soft.

Tucker grabs my wrists in a punishing grip. "Jensen," he barks.

One of his friends steps up behind me and buries a hand in my hair, yanking my head back at an awkward angle. The stinging pain makes me hiss and bend to keep the pressure off.

Tucker wraps his hand around my throat and digs his fingers in. "I'm going to—"

Whatever he planned to say is cut off by a dark growl. One second Tucker is glaring down at me and the next, a big body slams him into the wall with a thud that makes me wince.

*Everett.*

He's suddenly here, like some sort of superhero, punching Tucker until the cowboy's head snaps back against the brick and he slumps to the ground.

Everett turns on the man holding me tight. "Let her go or I'll put you down," he snarls.

That dark, sexy growl does something to me. I should not be turned on in this moment when there's five of them to two of us, but the low tug in my body is undeniable.

Jenkins tightens his hold. He nods to his friends. "Take care of him. Then we'll finish this."

They waste no time in ganging up on Everett.

I can't let them get away with this. Can't let Everett get hurt trying to help me. I dig my nails into the hands in my hair, but they aren't long enough to make much of an impact. My captor grunts and pulls my head back farther. The pain is excruciating and tears well in my eyes, blurring the fight.

Everett blocks their punches and kicks. One man lands a lucky punch to his side while another circles behind and wraps an arm around Everett's throat.

My heart clenches. This can't be happening.

Everett grips the arm at his throat for leverage, and leaps up to kick both feet into the man in front of him, sending him sprawling. The moment his boots touch the ground, he flips the one holding him over his shoulder and tosses him at the large green dumpsters. The third springs forward into the fray, crashing into Everett.

It happens so fast I can hardly breathe, and the tense body behind me tells me I'm not the only one enthralled by the fight.

Movement stirs behind them, and I see Tucker slowly getting to his feet. He shakes his head as if to clear it and reaches for a broken beer bottle laying next to him.

"No!" I can't let them hurt him, and I'm terrified of what Tucker might do to me if they overtake Everett. I have to help. Clenching my right hand, I slam my fist back, aiming for Jensen's groin. I hit something soft. He howls in pain and his fist loosens in my hair. I can't give him time to recover, so I stomp my foot down on his, then spin and punch him as hard as I can.

"Bitch," he spits as he goes down on one knee.

I kick him in the throat and don't feel an ounce of regret. These bullies have harassed me for six months. The second I can, I'm going to the sheriff. But first, I have to help Everett.

The yellow light over the diner's door flickers to life in the near darkness of the early evening, brought on by a timer. It illuminates the scene in vivid detail.

Two of the three men who fought Everett lie unmoving on the ground. The third writhes in agony, and the man I punched is coughing hard and gasping for breath. Only Tucker and Everett remain standing.

Tucker slashes at him with the broken bottle. Everett dodges and lands a punch that sends the cowboy staggering.

I scan the ground, looking for anything that I can use to help and spot a broken pallet nearby. I grab a piece of wood from it and turn back, ready to smash it over Tucker's head.

Before I can, he jabs the bottle at Everett.

Everett grabs Tucker's wrist and strikes it with his other hand. The bottle drops, shattering on the concrete, and Tucker cries out. He's forced to his knees as Everett twists his arm in an unnatural direction.

"You even look at her again, and it will be the last thing you ever do," Everett snarls at him.

"Fuck you," Tucker grunts.

"Remember what I said." He slams a fist in Tucker's face and the cowboy drops. Out. Cold.

Everett turns to me then, glancing at the piece of wood raised over my shoulder like a baseball bat. A ghost of a smile flickers on his lips. He strides forward, plucks my makeshift weapon out of my hands, and tosses it aside.

"Thank you."

I barely get the words out before he hauls me against his chest and slams his mouth down on mine.

# CHAPTER FIVE

## *Everett*

I haven't felt fear often. In the military, I quickly learned to detach myself from my emotions in tense situations so that I focused only on the mission. The moment I saw Tucker's crony restrain Lacey, ice slid down my spine and a dozen dark scenarios ran through my head of all the things that might happen before I could reach her. They're lucky they're still breathing.

Fire sears through my veins as I drop Tucker and turn toward Lacey. She has a piece of a pallet in hand, ready to bash someone, and the sight makes me smile. So fucking beautiful. I pluck the wood out of her hand, toss it, and yank her to me.

All thoughts of Tucker, and Seattle, and loneliness vanish as I press my lips to hers. There is nothing but Lacey.

The kiss is rough at first, hard and hungry, until her soft little moan penetrates my brain and I realize that I'm crushing her against me. I gentle the kiss and my hold. She's precious, and I'd never hurt her.

Lacey fists her hands in my shirt, pulling me closer, and opens to me.

She tastes sweet, like icing, and her sigh against my mouth is better than ambrosia as our tongues slide together.

A low groan sounds from behind me, reminding me that Lacey isn't safe yet.

I break the kiss and wrap my arm around her. Tucker and his friends are beginning to recoup, and I don't want Lacey anywhere near them. "Let's get you out of here." I usher her out of the alley onto Main Street. "Do you have a car?"

"No. I live only a few blocks away, so I normally walk to work."

Just the thought of Lacey walking to work every day in that sexy black button up dress that hugs her curves makes me want to toss her over my shoulder and head to the nearest car dealer. It's an insane thought, but nothing about my reaction to this woman makes sense. I'm done questioning it. If I've lost my fucking mind, so be it.

I steer her toward my truck and open the passenger side door. "Get in. I'll take you home."

Lacey shifts from foot to foot.

Shit, I didn't even think that she might be leery of me after that ordeal. What woman wouldn't be? I'm a stranger to her. "You can trust me, sweetheart. I give you my word that I'll take you straight home. You have nothing to fear. I just don't want you to walk home tonight when those assholes are injured and pissed. I couldn't live with myself if anything happened to you."

Her face softens. "Everett…"

I dig in my jeans pocket for the wood handle, open her palm, and wrap her fingers around the folded knife. "Here. Use it if you don't feel safe." I could take the knife off her before she got it open, but if it makes her feel safe with me, I'll give her every weapon I'm carrying.

"What? No." She tries to hand it back. "I'm not using a knife on you."

"Take it. I'm serious, Lacey. I need you home safe."

She frowns at me and stuffs the blade into her coat pocket, then climbs into my truck. "Fine. Take me home."

My instinct is to put the seatbelt on her, but she's had enough men in her personal space for one night—including me—so I hand it to her and she clicks it in. Probably should feel bad about kissing her, but I can't scrape up an ounce of regret. It's the best damn kiss I've ever had.

I climb in the driver's seat, start the engine, and crank up the heater, aiming the vents toward her.

"Thank you, Everett." Lacey takes my hand in hers as different emotions flicker through her eyes. Expressions of frustration, gratefulness, and fear. "I don't want to even t-think about what might have h-happened." Her voice cracks on the words and she trembles.

The need to pull her into my arms rides me hard. Instead, I say, "I saw the way he looked at you. There's no way in hell I'd allow him to hurt you." I can't resist brushing a stray lock of honey blonde hair behind her ear.

She leans into my touch.

The skin of her cheek is like silk beneath my fingers. "You good?"

"Yeah." She licks her lower lip.

I don't think she realizes how fucking tempting she is. How much I want to hold her, kiss her, and protect her. "I should get you home."

She nods and pulls away. Her breath catches when she sees the dash display. "Is that what time it is? I have to get home! Alice will be waiting."

I shouldn't be irritated that the moment is over since I'm the one who ended it, but here we are. "Point the way, sweetheart." I shift the truck into gear and follow her directions. There's no sign of the cowboys. "Who's Alice?"

"She's the nurse who helps my grandfather during the day."

"You care for him at night?" My respect for her rises another notch. It's difficult to care for an elderly relative and hold another job. My mother did once, and it broke her.

"It's nothing major. I make him dinner and we watch TV. Then I help him get ready for bed."

"How long have you been caring for him?"

"I moved here six months ago. Henry had fallen down the front steps and broken his leg. We couldn't afford to have a nurse with him at all hours, but he needed help. And I mean... I don't think he'd want to have strangers living with him."

God, she's sweet. "You must be pretty close to him."

"I am. Henry is my father's father. My dad died a few years ago. Mom's remarried and busy with her new family. She didn't want to deal with Henry's care. She was furious that I dropped out of college to move here, but he's my grandpa."

The pain in her voice tugs at my heart. "I'm sorry, Lacey. I think what you're doing is amazing."

Her lips tip up in a tiny smile. "Thanks. It's nice to know that someone does. Mom sure doesn't."

"Not all mothers can handle responsibility." The words come out harsher than they should.

"Are you close with your mom?"

I steal a glance at her. Would she pity me? Or understand? I war with myself on how to answer, and finally go with the truth. "No. My mother tried to care for my grandparents for a while. I guess it became too much to deal with. She split."

"She left you?"

The outrage in Lacey's tone spears something warm into my heart. "Right after I turned nine, I came home from school to find her note. She'd left us all behind."

"What happened to you?"

"My grandparents were all I had. I kept us going for a couple of weeks, making sandwiches and soup because I didn't know how to cook. It worked until my grandfather fell. He was too heavy to move." I scrub a hand down my face. "I had to call an ambulance to get him back into bed. It didn't take them long to realize the situation, and I went into foster care the next day."

"But you were her son. Why didn't she take you with her?"

"I've asked myself that a thousand times. After nine years in the system, I wanted no ties to her. As soon as I was out, I changed my last name to Smith, signed up for the military, and never looked back."

Lacey leans over to press a kiss to my stubbled cheek. "Her loss, because I think you're pretty special, Everett Smith."

My stomach bottoms out, and pressure fills my chest. Warmth blooms in its wake. A tenderness I've never felt before. Jesus, we're talking about something I've never told anyone else because it's fucking painful, yet I'm practically melting for this woman. I can't do this. I'm leaving tomorrow. "Are we close to your house?" My voice sounds like gravel.

A smile spreads over her plush lips. "Turn right at the next street."

Tall trees and Craftsman-style bungalows line the neighborhood. Lacey points to her house. I park in the driveway, then hustle around to open Lacey's door. It's natural to fit my hands to her waist and settle her against me until her feet touch the ground. The sweet scent of her hair fills my senses, and those tempting curves brush against my body.

Lacey leans into me. "Everett, would you stay for a little while?"

My hands slip around her waist. She's warm and soft, and holding her like this, I don't even notice the chill in the air. "You sure you haven't had enough of me?"

"Not possible," she whispers. Her head tilts back and those big, baby blue eyes find mine in the near darkness, reflecting the stars above.

Like magic, the world around us disappears, and the air grows thick between us. She fills my senses until all I can smell, see, and feel is Lacey, and yet we're still not close enough. This is madness. I can't get involved with her, and yet... "I want to kiss you again."

Lacey lifts on to her toes and presses her sweet mouth to mine.

Desire roars through me like a wildfire. I pull her closer and deepen the kiss. She melts against me. Her lips part beneath mine and our tongues slide together. The kiss is slow and tender, not the frenzied kiss from the alley. Somehow, that makes it sexier. I suck her lower lip between mine as I pull away, savoring a last taste.

Lacey moans. She's gripping my shirt in her fists, holding me to her. Our breath mingles in the space between our lips. "Stay. Please."

I shouldn't for many reasons. This connection, this feeling, it's like nothing I've ever known. When I think about taking that job in Seattle, it feels wrong. Yet staying gets me no closer to having a purpose. What the fuck am I doing?

"Please Everett?"

I stroke her hair away from her face. Tuck it behind her ear, savoring the feel of her skin. "I'll stay as long as you want, sweetheart." The words are out before I realize it. I press another soft kiss to her lips, giving in to fate for a few more hours.

The screen door creaks and a woman calls, "Lacey? Is that you?"

Lacey breaks the kiss and takes my hand. "Yes, Alice. Sorry I'm late. There's someone I want you and Henry to meet." She smiles up at me and pulls me toward the house.

I kick the truck door closed and follow her in. I'm starting to think I might follow this woman anywhere. But no, her life is here. Mine is waiting for me in Seattle. All the kisses in the world won't change that.

# CHAPTER SIX

## *Lacey*

Henry immediately liked Everett. They've spent the last two hours swapping stories about the military. I haven't seen my grandfather this happy, this animated, since I first came to White Falls. Everett's rich laugh rings out, making butterflies take flight in my stomach. God, that man. When I saw his full smile, my panties went damp. He's not just gorgeous, he's magnetic. And the more I learn about him, the more I like. He wants to protect people which is why he's taking the security job. He stands up to bullies and treats old men with respect and even admiration. How is it fair that he's just passing through?

Shaking my head, I collect the last of the dinner plates and take them to the kitchen. After Alice left, Everett helped me get Henry settled by the television, then wanted to help make dinner. He chopped vegetables and spoke a little about the loss he felt when he left the military. Not only leaving his friends behind, but feeling like he didn't know who he was anymore. My heart broke for him. He lost his family as a kid, and then the men in his unit became that family. He never said it, but I sense he's feeling as if he lost his family all over again.

I wonder about his new job. Will he make friends? Find a woman and start his own family? Does he want that?

My gaze returns to him. He's sitting on the couch with Henry, one arm on the back, while he listens to another story. The man is effortlessly gorgeous. His dark hair and those light gray eyes, the stubble on his jaw and those lips that kiss so well. The gray henley stretches across his broad shoulders, outlining the muscles. I bet he's still in as good of shape as he was on active duty. It's no hardship to imagine pulling his shirt off and running my hands over his chest. I know it's impossible that he will stay. It doesn't stop me from wishing he would, but he'd have to want to stay here. With me.

My stomach flip-flops at the thought. I've never felt this way with anyone. Especially after so short a time. Does he feel it too? Could there ever be a time and place where we could be more? I can't leave Henry, and the idea of a long-distance relationship has never appealed to me. But maybe one day after Henry is gone...

My throat gets thick, and I have to turn away. Don't want either of them to see me get emotional about a love that probably has zero chance anyway.

The thing is, Everett is everything that I've ever dreamed of. He's caring, tender, and so protective. I think I started falling for him before I left the diner. Since I almost fell in his lap and pressed my boobs in his face like a weirdo. When he fought for me, putting Tucker in his place, he rescued me from a situation that could have ended badly. How could he not get to my heart?

I feel the warmth of him before I hear his voice.

"Need help?" His low words whisper in my ear, making me tremble with desire. I want him to say naughty things to me in that dark, sexy voice while he's pushing inside me.

Everett's hand lands on my waist, anchoring me against that delicious chest. "I want everything you have to give." The words slip out before I realize that

I'm going to say them, but I wouldn't take them back even if I could. I mean them with every fiber of my being and not just his help with the dishes. I want Everett Smith forever. So tragic, because tomorrow he's driving out of my life and not coming back.

Tears sting my eyes and I blink them back as rapidly as possible, hoping he doesn't see. I don't want to explain. How do you tell a man you just met that you think you're in love with him and want him to stay? It sounds crazy.

His lips ghost over my temple. "Careful, sweetheart. I might take you up on that."

I huff out an awkward laugh. I won't let tears ruin our time together. "Enjoy talking to Henry?"

Everett's hand smooths over my hip and up my side in soothing strokes. "Very much. Old-timers like him have a different take on life. They saw a lot during the wars. Things only men like me can relate to. Thank you, Lacey. Talking with him, telling stories, it reminded me why it's important to stay in contact with the men of my old unit. They're the only family I have. I can't turn my back on them. I need them, and I think they need me."

I turn in his arms and search his face. The vulnerability in his eyes is staggering. I never thought I'd see it in such a strong man, and it only makes me crave him more. Wrapping my arms around his waist, I lay my head on his chest. "I'm glad I could give something back to you. It will never be enough to thank you for what you did today."

He tips my chin up and rubs his thumb over my lips. His kiss is tender and far too short. Henry coughs from the living room, breaking the spell.

Everett's lips twitch. "Let me help."

"No. I've got this. Spend a few more minutes with Henry. He'll probably be ready for bed soon."

"Let me take care of him. After that, maybe we can talk more."

I'll take any time I can get. I make quick work of cleaning up dinner and then hug Henry goodnight. The look my grandfather gives me is pure love.

"She's good to me, Everett. Puts up with a lot. Even quit college to come help me. Not many women would give up something like that to spend hours with a ninety-year-old man." Henry squeezes my hand.

"She is special," Everett says. When our eyes lock, his look is intense.

I wish I could read his expression to know what he's feeling.

"Sure is. She needs a man to love and protect her. Help her dreams come true."

A blush hits me so fast, my cheeks feel like they're on fire. "Grandpa!"

Henry laughs. "She only 'grandpa's' me when I embarrass her."

Everett winks at me, a smile tugging at his lips. "Let's get you to bed, old timer." He pushes Henry's wheelchair into his bedroom, and the door clicks behind them.

I spend a few minutes cleaning up the house to keep myself busy. As I fold Henry's lap blanket, I realize I'm still in my work dress. I should shower. I should shave! Do I have anything sexy to wear? Would Everett want to see me in something sexy?

He comes out of Henry's room, intercepting me before I can rifle through my entire wardrobe.

"Henry's settled in bed. Where you rushing off to, sweetheart?" He catches my hand and draws me back to his side.

"I've worn this all day, so I was going to change." I wave at the black button-down dress and then scrub at a gravy stain on the skirt.

"Mmm, I like it. The way it hugs your body…"

Startled, I search his face and find the heat I hoped to see. His eyes skim down my body and a rumbling noise comes from his chest that makes me press my thighs together. I hope I'm not reading this wrong. Before I can overthink it, I press my lips to his.

Everett's growl vibrates against my lips as he wraps his arms around me and backs me against the wall.

My head bumps into a picture frame, but I don't care. Winding my arms around his neck, I pull him closer and open to him. The kiss is hot, primal, and… we're right outside Henry's room. The thought pulls me out of the passion, like being doused in ice water. "Henry."

Everett seems to understand. He takes my hand and leads me back into the living room. He sinks down onto the couch, pulling me onto his lap.

"Wait, I'm too—"

He covers my protest with a kiss. Nips at my lower lip. "You're not too heavy, Lacey. You're perfect. This," his hands slide over my shoulders, down my arms, to my sides. "This body is perfect."

Any protest I might have made evaporates under another intense kiss. There are a hundred reasons why this is a bad idea and I don't care about any of them. If this is all I get of Everett Smith, I want it. I want him.

"I want you too, Lacey," he whispers against my lips.

I hadn't realized I said the words aloud. Threading my fingers through his hair, I pull his mouth to mine. The kiss is electric, lighting up my body in a way I've never felt before. My hard nipples rub against the satin of my bra, and my core is damp and aching for him. "Touch me," I pant against his mouth.

"With pleasure," Everett breathes, his hands molding against my hips before gliding upwards to cup my breasts, his touch both tender and possessive. He pinches my nipples through the fabric, and a bolt of desire shoots to my core.

My hips grind against his hard cock, driving my pleasure higher.

"That's it. Take what you want." He opens the first few buttons on my dress and slides his hand inside to cup my breast. "Need to see these."

In seconds, my dress is unbuttoned and bunched at my waist. Everett presses a kiss between my breasts, then unhooks my black satin bra. The sound he makes is almost animalistic as his mouth closes over one of my hard peaks, his hand pinching the other.

"So fucking gorgeous, Lacey." He licks and sucks and nips at my breasts until I'm writhing on his lap. One of his hands slides lower and delves between my legs.

Only then do I realize that he's completely supporting me in his arms. He's bent me back over the arm banded around me to feast on my breasts, anchoring me to his lap while the other hand slips into my panties.

"Wet for you," I murmur.

He hums in agreement and strokes his hand through my folds. "Shit, Lacey. You're going to make me come. The way you move is so sexy. I've never been this hard."

I capture his lips in another kiss, saying without words everything that's in my heart. The way he makes me feel, his sweet words and protective nature, the way he cares for Henry... I think I'm in love with him.

Everett lifts his head to search my eyes. A small smile touches his lips before he places a tender kiss against my mouth. "I want you to come for me, sweetheart."

His fingers dip to my entrance, sliding through my slick folds. One finger pushes into me. Two. His thumb finds my clit. Then he's working his fingers into me while circling his thumb. Over and over. Pushing me higher and higher.

I bite my lip hard to keep quiet.

"That's it, baby. Ride my hand. Let go."

A flick of his thumb sends me careening over the edge. I bury my head against his neck to muffle my moans as I come in the strongest orgasm I've ever had.

Everett slows his strokes, bringing me down. "Beautiful." His kiss is tender. "Next time, I'm getting my mouth on all of this gorgeous skin first and make you ride my tongue."

His hot words send a tiny aftershock through me. "Next time?"

The second the words are out of my mouth, I realize that I've made a mistake.

Everett tenses beneath me. He withdraws his hand from between my thighs and pulls my dress back into place.

The sweet fizz of pleasure disappears, replaced with a chill that goes straight to my bones. Suddenly, I feel like I can't get warm.

The regret in his eyes is more than I can deal with. It hurts. I knew I couldn't keep him. I knew it would be painful when he left. But I never expected *his* remorse to slash at me worse than a knife.

I stand on shaking legs, unsure what to do or say. I don't want to cry. Not yet.

"I'm sorry, Lacey. I should never have let things go this far. It's not fair to you.

Your heart is too precious to be toyed with."

I can't hear over the buzzing in my ears, so I nod.

His forehead wrinkles as he stands. "Lacey?"

"Just go." I shouldn't kick him out. It's late and I don't know if he'll be able to get a room at the motel. I should offer him the couch, but the words won't come. All that's left is hurt. I'm such an idiot. I fell in love with a man I knew I would never see again after tomorrow. Maybe he feels guilty right now. All I know is that my feelings, the heartache, they're my fault. I knew better than to get attached, and I did anyway.

Everett lifts a hand as if to cup my cheek, then quickly pulls it back. "We'll talk tomorrow. I'm not leaving town until we do."

I'm not sure if I agreed or not. All I can hear are the swirling recriminations in my head.

Everett gives me one last look, then heads out into the night. The thump of the closing door echoes in my heart.

# CHAPTER SEVEN
## *Everett*

I checked into the motel, but I couldn't sleep. Every time I closed my eyes, all I saw was the hurt on Lacey's face. She knew I was passing through, that I was leaving tomorrow, so it isn't as if I deceived her, but that's not what kept me up. It was the knowledge that she is just as caught up in these feelings as I am. The hurt I saw reflected exactly what I felt. What I still feel. I don't regret touching and kissing her. I regret that doing so hurt her, and I wonder if she understood that when I left.

Unlikely.

I paced the room until well after dawn. No magic solutions revealed themselves. I need to talk to Lacey. I just don't know what I'm going to say.

Dragging myself into the shower, I dip my head under the hot water and try to think. We just met. It's madness that I would have such strong feelings for her already. I've never believed in love at first sight. Hell, I barely believe in love at all.

And Lacey is young. She just dropped out of college. There has to be an age gap of at least eleven or twelve years between us, not to mention life experience. Fuck, my head's still a mess from leaving the military behind. What will happen when she no longer takes care of Henry? I didn't get the chance to ask her what her dreams were.

Whatever they are, I'll support them.

My head jerk up at the thought and water sprays me in the face. I rub a hand over it to clear the water from my eyes and lean back into the spray, letting it pound my shoulders.

It doesn't matter how I try to deny it; I want Lacey. Now and forever. The age gap, the location, none of that matters to my heart, apparently. But I've committed to the security company in Seattle. I haven't signed the contract yet, but I've submitted all the background checks and additional forms to start. If I were to stay in White Falls, breaking the agreement would hurt me professionally. That might not be so bad, but what would I do here? I doubt there are many foreign dignitaries or celebrities passing through White Falls in need of security. If I don't have a job, I can't take care of Lacey. I need the financial stability for her to follow her dreams, whatever they are.

A dozen scenarios run through my head and none of them offer any hope. I can't stay right now, and she can't come with me. There's no way to make a long distance relationship work if I'm all over the world for extended periods of time. That was part of the contract that appealed to me. Now, there's only one place I want to be—beside Lacey. There's just... no way out of this.

I smack my hand against the shower valve to turn it off and step out to dry and dress. I have to see her. We can't leave things like this. I just wish I knew where we go from here.

It's almost eight thirty by the time I get to Gravy Lane. The breakfast crowd packs the diner and the smell of bacon wafts from within. My girl should be in there. Instead, she standing at the mouth of the alley, talking to the sheriff.

With her arms crossed and fists clenched, she appears vulnerable and on edge.

"Lacey." She looks up when I join her, but her smile is strained and doesn't reach her eyes. "You okay?" I want to put my arm around her to offer comfort, but I don't know if she'd welcome it.

"Fine."

She sounds anything but fine, but I can't ask her more out here. The sheriff introduces himself, and Lacey explains how I stepped in to help her when the cowboy and his friends were intimidating her.

There's a glint of humor in the man's eye when he looks me over. "You the one that gave Colby Tucker that black eye?"

"Along with a few bruises." It's no secret that there was a fight. Not gonna sugar coat it when I was defending Lacey.

"Wish I could have witnessed it," the man murmurs. "He's needed to be knocked down a couple of notches for a long time. Can you come by my office to give a statement?"

I glance at Lacey but can't read her expression. "Yes. I'll be in town at least another day. Maybe longer."

Her eyebrows raise, but she doesn't comment.

The sheriff scribbles something in his notepad and snaps it shut. "I'll be there until five. Lacey, you pressing charges?"

She shifts, looking uncomfortable. "Only if Tucker won't leave me alone."

"We can help you get a restraining order against him. Once people hear about this, he'll have a rough time around town."

"That won't be necessary," a man says from behind me.

His voice is familiar, but I'm too pissed at myself for not being more aware of my surroundings to recognize it right away. How can I keep Lacey—or anyone—safe if someone can sneak up behind me? I turn to the newcomer and the voice clicks. "Caleb Dalton."

The cropped blond hair he had during our missions has grown out a bit, but he's still in peak form, judging by the way he moves. He offers me his hand. I take it, noting the faces of the two men standing behind him. One is Colby Tucker. The other is one of his friends from last night.

"Good to see you, Smith. Didn't know you'd discharged."

"A couple of months back. These two with you?" I nod at Tucker. The cowboy looks away. There's anger in his stance, but he's subdued for now.

"Yet to be seen," Caleb replies. He nods to the sheriff, then holds up a pink box he's carrying to Lacey. "An apology, courtesy of Harmony."

The sheriff groans. "Your wife's pastries are the reason I have to diet now."

Caleb grins and opens the lid to show a variety of sweets inside.

Wife? Sure enough, there's a wedding band on Caleb's finger.

Lacey hesitates. "You have nothing to be sorry for, Mr. Dalton."

"Maybe not, but these two do. They've been working for me while I get my family's ranch up and running again. Except I don't tolerate intimidation and bullying, especially toward women." Dalton catches my eye, and I know we're both thinking about the missions we shared. What humanity does to one another is unfathomable, and we saw hundreds of women and children abused at the hands of those who should protect them. Those missions burned a code in all of us to protect, always.

"Sorry, Lacey," Tucker mutters, not meeting her eye. "We'll leave you alone. I swear."

"Thanks."

I'm burning to gather her in my arms, but keep my distance.

The sheriff claps Dalton on the shoulder, then shares a private word with the cowboys, who look contrite. "These boys are coming back with me to give their statements. You can pick them up there."

"Right behind you," Dalton says. He spears me with a look. "I'm shocked as hell to see you, man. How'd you end up in White Falls?"

"Wrong turn." Caleb laughs at that and I fight a grin. We were pretty close once. It's good to see him. "I was on my way to Seattle to take a security gig."

His gaze flicks to Lacey and back. "If you should change your mind about that, let me know. I do some work for Citadel Securities, which Gideon Blake owns. He's looking for more people. Let's grab a beer before you go, okay?"

I agree, and we clasp forearms. A sense of belonging sweeps over me. He might not be my blood brother, but he's family in all the ways that count. For the first time in months, I feel at peace. I know what I have to do.

Dalton apologizes again to Lacey, makes her take the pastries, and kisses her cheek. With a final nod at me, he follows after the sheriff and Tucker.

Lacey stares at the box as if she doesn't know what to do with it.

"Those smell good."

"Harmony makes some of the best pastries in town. It was kind of Mr. Dalton to bring me some."

"You all done with the sheriff?"

"Yes, and my boss heard what happened yesterday. He insisted I go home and rest." She finally looks at me. "I'm not sure what I should do."

Her words say she's uncertain about taking the day off, but the tightness of her posture and those sweet lips tell a different story.

Slowly, I reach for her free hand, giving her time to step away. She threads her fingers with mine. "Let's find a place to eat those, then I need to make a call."

# CHAPTER EIGHT
## *Lacey*

Everett and I walk down to the park near the town square. I sit on a bench under a big cedar tree and snack on an apple fritter while he moves away to make his call. A huge yawn escapes me. I barely slept last night, tossing and turning as I thought over every moment, every touch and conversation with Everett, wondering if I could have done anything different to make him fall in love with me. To get him to stay. It felt like I barely fell asleep when the alarm went off, and my sluggish brain hasn't caught up.

I'm still not exactly certain why I have a box of pastries from Layered Love, but I'm not complaining. Harmony makes the best turnovers, cupcakes, and donuts that I've ever had. She had a stalker for a time, and it was Caleb who helped her. They ended up falling in love.

I sneak a glance at Everett. A light breeze ruffles his dark hair as he finishes his call. He's so hot. And when he smiles like he did last night with Henry, he's devastating. As if sensing my thoughts, he looks my way and flashes a smile, then tucks his phone back in his pocket.

"Did you save one for me?" he asks as he joins me.

I dig out a crumb from the corner of the box and hand it to him.

Everett laughs and the deep, happy sound washes through me, tugging an answering smile from my mouth.

He bends down and presses a kiss to my temple. "That's okay, sweetheart," he whispers in my ear. "There's something else I want for breakfast that I think will taste even better."

"Everett—"

"I love you, Lacey."

My mouth drops open. Of all the things I expected he might say, that was nowhere near the list. "I... what?"

He sits on the bench and cups my cheeks with his warm palms. "I'm in love with you, Lacey. I know we just met and things moved fast, but I loved you from the moment you came to my table."

I huff a laugh. "Was that when I tackled you in the booth and gave you an eyeful?" God, I'm so embarrassed about that.

He grins. "Before, but having my arms full of a gorgeous, curvy woman with great tits was further confirmation."

I bite my lip. "What about Seattle?"

"I called to tell them I'm not taking the job."

My tummy flips over, and butterflies erupt inside. I'm so afraid to hope.

"Your life is here, and I realized I couldn't leave. Not without you. But how could I be the man you needed if I couldn't provide for you? Running into Dalton was the answer." He tucks a stray strand of hair back behind my ear. "None of that matters though, if you don't feel the same. I love you, Lacey."

My eyes prick with tears and this time, I let them fall. "I love you too, Everett."

He kisses my tears, then crushes his mouth to mine. The kiss tastes like apple and the sweetest love.

When we break apart, his eyes glint with promise. "Come with me, sweetheart. You owe me breakfast."

I hold up the box of pastries and bite back a grin, though my heart wants to soar. "I have more."

"Not what I meant." Everett scoops me into his arms as if I weigh nothing and carries me to his truck. He holds my hand the entire way back to the motel, like he's scared I'll vanish. And once we get there, he practically sprints to his room, dragging me along.

As soon as the door closes behind us, Everett pulls me into his arms and slants his mouth over mine. The kiss is hot and possessive, needy, and my core floods with heat.

He rips his shirt over his head and drops it behind him, then starts unbuttoning my pink dress. It gives me time to admire his hard body. I run my hands over the planes of his chest, marveling at the definition. His arms are like rocks and his abs are perfection.

"I wanted you so badly last night, Lacey. I wanted to peel that dress off you and bury my tongue between your thighs until you screamed my name, but Henry was there."

"He's not here now."

Everett slips the last button open on my dress and pushes it off my shoulders. I have the tiniest flash of nerves, but the raw desire on his face quickly chases it away.

"Fuck me, you're gorgeous. I love that black lace bra, but I don't trust myself not to rip it. Take it off. I want to see those beautiful breasts."

Unhooking the bra, I slide the straps down my arms, then slowly peel it away.

Everett sinks to his knees and cups my breasts. "Perfection," he murmurs and sucks one nipple into his mouth.

The wet heat makes my knees weak, and I sway against him.

Switching to the other breast, he sucks lightly, and then guides me backward until I hit the bed. He swats my ass. "Get in."

I climb in and lie back, watching him remove the rest of his clothes.

When he's finally bare, Everett crawls over my body and gives me a hard kiss. "Say it again," he murmurs against my lips.

"I love you, Everett."

"That's my girl. Now open those pretty legs. I'm going to lick you until you scream my name."

Heart pounding in anticipation, I do as he says.

Everett dips his fingers in the sides of my panties and yanks them down my legs. He strokes my skin almost reverently. "You're mine, sweetheart."

I love the way his voice grows rough with desire. The way he looks at me as if I'm someone to be cherished.

He settles his broad shoulders between my thighs, leans close, blows a warm breath over my core.

"Everett!"

# CHAPTER NINE
### *Everett*

My mouth is watering for a taste of her pretty pink pussy. Parting her lips, I savor this moment, then trace her with the tip of my tongue. She tastes divine. I could do this forever.

Lacey's fingers spear into my hair and she tugs me closer, silently demanding more.

I lick her from her core to her clit, avoiding the place she wants me most. I suck, lick, and nip her folds, stroking my tongue through that sweetness and lapping at her until she's bucking against my mouth. So fucking good.

"Oh god, Everett. D-don't stop..."

Oh, I have no intention of that. I work her until she's panting, writhing, almost riding my face. Then I suck her clit into my mouth and she explodes, crying out my name. I lick her until she settles back on the bed, savoring every drop.

"Everett, please. I need to feel you. I need you inside me." Her voice is breathy, and she squirms beneath me.

I raise up over her, planting a hand on either side of her head and line my dick up with her entrance. "Guide me in, love."

Lacey wraps her hand around my cock, and I jolt in her hand. Too much of that and I'll come before I get inside her. My tip brushes her wet folds. "Christ, you're soaked."

"Only for you."

Her words are the sweetest music. Lining up, I push inside her hot pussy and moan in ecstasy. I'm only halfway in and this is already better than any sex I've ever had. She's tight and every inch causes a wave of pleasure to wash over me. When I'm fully seated, I can't wait. I pull back a touch, then thrust into her hot channel.

Lacey cries out my name and wraps her legs around my hips, drawing me closer. I thrust into her, over and over. She meets my every stroke. Her nails bite into my skin, and the slight sting pushes me over the edge. My hips snap back, then I slam into her, again and again.

"Come for me, sweetheart. I need to feel you milk me."

"Everett!" Lacey bucks beneath me, her core gripping me tight, and the orgasm sweeps her under.

Pleasure is like hot lava, building up pressure in my spine. I come with a force that makes me sway. When the last tremor subsides, I collapse to the bed beside her and pull her into my arms.

We fight to catch our breath and it's a couple of minutes until I can form coherent thoughts.

"What happens now?" Lacey asks into the quiet of the room.

I roll to my side and prop my head on my palm. She faces me, and I see the concern and the lingering doubt in her eyes.

We may not have known each other long, but this connection is real. I found a once in a lifetime love with Lacey. I'd be a fool to let her go.

"Now I take you up on your offer." I lift her hand and place a kiss on her finger, where I plan to put my engagement ring as soon as possible.

"What offer?"

"You said you wanted everything I have to give. I plan to stay until it's yours. I love you, Lacey. Now, and forever."

# Epilogue
## *Everett*

*Two Months Later*

"Are you sure this is what you want, son?"

I put a hand on Henry's thin shoulder and give it a gentle squeeze. "I've never been more certain of anything." There's a hush to the church vestibule that makes this moment feel sacred. String music plays just beyond the heavy wood doors where Lacey's friends and some of my brothers from the military wait. I pushed Henry's wheelchair out here so he could wait for Lacey. "You look good in a tux, old timer."

Henry grins. "Think Alice will give me a dance?"

I chuckle. "Sure she will." Henry's been flirting with his home health nurse for years and it's cute as fuck to watch.

The old man turns serious, and he reaches for my hand. "I know you'll take good care of my Lacey. Anyone with eyes can see how much you love her. But I want you to know how honored I am that you're taking our family name."

His words tug at my heart. My throat feels thick, and it's a minute or two before I can speak. "When I turned eighteen, I changed my last name to Smith because I didn't want any ties to my mother or my family. You and Lacey are my family, Henry. I'm the one that's honored because you're letting me be a part of it. Besides, Everett Armstrong sounds damn good."

Henry wipes at a tear in his eye. "That it does, son. Now, go take your place. Lacey will be out any minute." He pats my hand and then shoos me toward the doors.

This man has become both father and grandfather to me, and the love he's given me fills a void in my heart I didn't know I had. He and Lacey are everything to me, and in a few minutes, they will officially be mine.

I stride through the wooden doors and down the aisle, nodding to Caleb's wife, Harmony, who sits next to Gideon Blake and his girlfriend. Turns out Harmony is Gideon's sister. I had a great time giving Caleb shit about taking his life in his hands by falling in love with her. It's been good to reconnect with them, and with some of the other men I deployed with, and I'm reminded that the family you choose can be better than the family you're born to.

"Ready?" the pastor asks as I join him at the front of the church.

"Never been more ready." I straighten my tuxedo jacket and shirt cuffs, but I'm not nervous. I would have made Lacey my wife the day after I claimed her, but she wanted a church wedding. I'd give her anything, so here we are.

Caleb steps up beside me, looking distracted. He pats one pocket, then another, then checks his inner jacket pocket. "Was I supposed to have the rings?"

I shake my head. "You better not have lost them, fucker."

He chuckles and takes a velvet box out of his jacket. "We're good. Just had to give you shit. I'm glad you stayed, man. Citadel Securities is an excellent company to work with and I appreciate your help on the ranch."

I took Caleb up on his offer and joined Citadel. The security company protects people, rescues hostages... all the things we trained for in Delta Force. It feels good to use my skills, and because the missions can be anywhere, I don't have to live in New Orleans where the main office is located. I live with Lacey and Henry, and work with Caleb in between missions, learning how to raise cattle.

I'm going to have a bigger house built soon. Lacey doesn't know it yet, but I already bought property out near Caleb's. Lacey and Harmony are good friends, and I want our kids to grow up together. As soon as Lacey's ready, I want to put a baby in her belly. I can't wait to see her round with our child. To show the baby all the love a parent should.

"Holy shit. It's Ezra."

Caleb's startled words bring me out of my thoughts and I look up to see a man with auburn hair and a full beard take a seat in the very back row, near the door. Ezra was medically discharged from our unit over a year ago after an accident damaged his brain and he dropped off the radar. It's a relief to see him here.

Ezra gives me a nod.

"Gideon must have found him," Caleb adds. "He said he was renting their family cabin to someone."

"He certainly looks like a mountain man." If Ezra is staying nearby, I want to spend some time with him. Like Caleb and Gideon, these men were all I had for years. They're my brothers and I've missed them more than I realized.

The pastor coughs politely and murmurs, "It's time."

The string music changes to Lacey's favorite piano tune, and my heart picks up speed. Everyone turns to face the doors, and when they open again, a vision of perfection steps through.

My heart stops, then pounds in earnest.

Lacey's white lace dress clings to every gorgeous curve, the spots between the lace hinting at the fair skin beneath. She holds Henry's hand, walking beside his wheelchair that Alice pushes down the aisle.

Our gazes lock as she comes toward me, and in her eyes I see the future. This woman is mine, and I'm thankful every day that I took a wrong turn all those weeks ago. I'm lost for her. There's nowhere else I'd rather be than by Lacey's side. Forever.

Thank you for reading Everett and Lacey's story. I hope you loved it! Want to learn more about Caleb and Harmony? Read their story in Fighting for Harmony, in the Strength and Honor charity anthology.

# Also by Ash Henry

**Citadel Securities Series**
If You're Mine
Claim You're Mine
Fighting for Harmony


**White Falls**
Lost For You
His to Unwrap

# About the Author

Ash Henry writes the contemporary romance she loves to read: sexy heroes who fall fast and hard, women who fight for what they want, and sizzling heat. Also, military men, age gap, action, love at first sight, families you make, and always a happily ever after. When she's not writing those swoony stories, she's reading them, with a cup of coffee in hand.

www.ingramcontent.com/pod-product-compliance
Lightning Source LLC
Chambersburg PA
CBHW070949120726
47910CB00004B/1170